A Second Chance Road Trip for Christmas

Holidays with the Wongs, Book 2

Jackie Lau

First edition: November 2019

Print ISBN: 978-1-989610-41-1

Editor: Latoya C. Smith, LCS Literary Services

Cover Design: Flirtation Designs

Chapter 1

"I have a special request," Greg's mom said.

Greg Wong sighed and put the nature documentary on mute. He was pretty sure he would not like his mother's request.

"What is it?" he asked, clutching the phone to his ear.

"I want you to drive Tasha Edwards back to Mosquito Bay for the Christmas holidays. You're getting off work early and leaving Monday afternoon, right?"

It took Greg a moment to find his voice. "Yes."

But he hated it when people changed his plans on him. He loved plans. He made meticulous plans whenever he could.

"Wonderful!" Mom said. "She'll meet you at your condo at three, okay?"

"Why am I driving her home for the holidays?"

"I met her mother at the grocery store the other day—they had an amazing sale on prime rib, so we're going to have a roast when you get home on the twenty-third, what do you think? And she mentioned that Tasha's car had broken down and she hadn't gotten around to buying a new one yet. Since it's hard to get to Mosquito Bay without a car and you're already making the drive from Toronto, I figured, why not?"

Greg took off his glasses and pinched the bridge of his nose.

Dear God.

He'd been looking forward to driving back to his hometown alone. His plan was to listen to CBC Radio, enjoy the solitude, and prepare himself for his boisterous family.

Now it was being snatched away from him.

Instead, he'd be spending hours in the car with his ex-girlfriend.

There were no hard feelings between him and Tasha, though. He'd known her since they were children, and she was the first girl he'd ever loved. They'd started dating in high school when they were sixteen and parted on amicable terms when they were in university, after nearly three years of dating.

God, it had been fifteen years since they'd been together. A lifetime ago.

He hadn't thought he'd still be single at thirty-four, but he found the whole dating business difficult and usually spent Saturday nights at home, watching Hockey Night in

Canada and working on his model railway, which wasn't a great way to meet women.

So when his parents had set him up with a woman at Thanksgiving, Greg—unlike his siblings—hadn't minded. Lily was nice, but before he'd really gotten to know her, it became apparent that she and his brother Nick had a history, and now they were in a relationship.

And Greg suspected that the main reason his mother was asking him to drive Tasha home was because she wanted to set them up.

"Mom, I'm not getting back together with my ex."

"Who said anything about that?" Mom said, but she wasn't fooling him. "I just want you to drive her back for the holidays, nothing more."

He grunted.

There was no good reason to refuse. If Tasha met him at his condo, it wouldn't be inconvenient for him at all, and her parents' house was only three blocks from where his own parents lived. *I want to listen to CBC Radio in peace* wasn't the sort of excuse that people understood, and if he said no, his mother would keep bugging him about it. She'd call him every few hours until he agreed. When she got an idea in her head, she wouldn't let go of it.

Best to just accept it.

He was driving home for Christmas with his high school sweetheart.

·❤·❤·❤·❤·❤·

On Monday December 23 at 3:01, Greg was sitting in the lobby of his building, waiting for Tasha. She should have been here sixty-two seconds ago.

Not that he'd hold being a minute late against anyone, but she'd just sent him a text from Davisville Station, which meant it would take her another twenty minutes to get here.

Hmph.

Tasha was usually on time. She wasn't one of those people who was always running late—like his sister—but she wasn't as obsessive about time as he was.

At least, that's what she'd been like before. He supposed he didn't really know her anymore. He'd seen her only a handful of times since their break-up—all at get-togethers with mutual friends—and the last time had been five years ago.

Greg was particularly anxious about the time today. He wanted to get out of the city well before five, not only because of the traffic, but because a snowstorm was supposed to hit later this evening. He wanted to be in Mosquito Bay by then, eating prime rib and listening to his family squabble.

Except Tasha was screwing up his plans, dammit.

Finally, at 3:27, she entered the lobby of his building, a big smile on her face. She pulled off her toque, and her braids tumbled about her face, and oh God, what was wrong with him? His heart was beating quickly—had he developed a heart condition?

No, this fluttering was just what happened when she was around. Apparently his body was still conditioned to respond this way, even though he hadn't seen her in years.

She'd been very pretty as a teenager, and she was very pretty now as a woman. She looked different, though. He couldn't explain exactly how, but she did.

She grinned even wider when she saw him. "It's good to see you, Greg."

His brain suddenly emptied, and he was unable to do anything but grunt.

Tasha didn't seem bothered by his lack of clear speech, however. That wasn't surprising—she'd always been able to interpret his grunts, even when he wasn't sure what they meant. It was one of her superpowers.

"You're late," he said gruffly.

"I'm so sorry. I got tied up at work. I told my boss I was leaving early, but we were trying to finish something up before the holidays and…well, what are we waiting for? Let's go!"

Greg had a feeling this was going to be a very long trip.

He just hoped the traffic and weather co-operated.

Tasha really was sorry about being late. She'd wanted to get out of the office at a good time, excited about seeing her parents for Christmas, but she took her job very seriously. It was the best one she'd had since she'd graduated.

As an aerospace engineer, she was used to being surrounded by men, and at her last workplace, she'd felt like she was always left out and passed over for things, but this job was good. She did aerodynamic modeling at a company that specialized in wind tunnel testing for buildings. It wasn't what she'd initially thought she'd do with her degrees, but she enjoyed it. Though it was a quieter office than she'd prefer—not much chit-chat around the coffeemaker or anything like that—everyone was kind and respected her.

Greg was an engineer, too. As he took her suitcase, she looked at his right hand and saw the iron ring on his pinky, just like hers.

She followed him into the elevator and down to the parking garage.

"Thank you so much for driving me back to Mosquito Bay," she said.

He grunted in acknowledgement.

Well, he really hadn't changed much, had he?

Except he'd filled out a bit since he was a teenager. Even in his winter jacket, she could see the difference.

"I could have taken the train," she continued, "but it's a long ways for my parents to go into London to pick me up, and you're driving to Mosquito Bay anyway, so it's not like you have to go out of your way. Though if it hadn't been for me, you'd have left half an hour ago."

"Yes."

She hurried to match his long strides. "Like I said, I'm sorry."

"It's fine."

He clearly wasn't happy, but apologizing again wasn't going to help.

"Nick lives in Toronto, too, doesn't he?"

"Yeah, he's some kind of hotshot executive."

She laughed. "Nick? Really?" Greg's brother, the one closest in age to them, had been a bit awkward in school.

"Yeah. And he was quite the playboy, up until a few months ago."

She struggled to wrap her mind around that. "What happened a few months ago?"

"He met a woman. Fell in love. You know." Greg stopped in front of a red Camry. "Get in. I'll put your suitcase in the trunk."

"My car is a Camry, too!" she said, then sighed, deflated. "Well, it was. It's gone now. My dad got it for me second-hand after I finished undergrad. Much older than your Camry, but I loved it."

He popped open the trunk and gave her a look.

"Oh, right! I should get inside!" She hurried to the passenger's seat and sat down. "Okay, I'm ready."

He sat down next to her and started the car without a word.

She had a feeling this was going to be a very long trip.

Chapter 2

GREG WAS IN THE car with the woman he'd once thought he'd marry, and she was driving him bananas. First she'd been late, and now she was talking. A lot.

Truth be told, he'd liked that about her before. He'd always found it difficult to string together more than a couple sentences and had admired how easy it was for her. He'd liked how she could keep the conversation going without too much effort on his part, and if he'd wanted, he could always kiss her to make her stop talking.

But not now. Because he was driving.

Plus, that wasn't the way things were between them anymore.

It had been over a decade and he was totally over Tasha. Of course he was. But since they hadn't spent any time alone together since breaking up, it was weird to be in his car with her, just the two of them.

His car.

When they'd dated, they hadn't owned cars. They hadn't had careers. Now, they were proper grown-ups.

Yeah, this was just plain weird.

It was a blast from the past, and it felt all wrong.

"...anyway," Tasha was saying, "let's liven things up a little."

Those were some of Greg's least favorite words in the English language, right up there with any phrase involving the word "party."

The absolute worst? Surprise parties.

Greg liked to prepare himself for long periods of forced socialization. He'd had only two days' notice for this driving-Tasha-back-to-Mosquito-Bay business. It wasn't enough, and his careful plans to get to his hometown before the snowstorm hit were crumbling. There was already a snowflake on his windshield, even though the snow wasn't supposed to begin for another hour.

The radio was telling him about the many traffic problems around the city and warning of the impending storm and—

Wait a second. Why had "Deck the Halls" started playing in the middle of the forecast?

"*Fa la la la la,*" Tasha sang, "*la la la la!*"

No. This couldn't be happening. Where was his beloved CBC Radio One?

"Come on, Greg!" she said. "Where's your Christmas spirit?"

He growled in frustration.

"'Tis the season to be jolly…"

It was impressive, really. She still knew exactly how to push his buttons.

"Did you pair your phone with my car's Bluetooth?" he asked in horror. "I need to listen to the traffic report."

"No, you don't. The traffic sucks. You don't need a report to tell you that."

"I have to know which route to take."

"I've got Google Maps open on my phone. The 401 is still moving, it's just slow."

"If you hadn't been twenty-seven minutes late, we wouldn't have hit such heavy traffic."

She shrugged. "Don't worry so much."

She was right. He did worry too much at times. But he couldn't help being afraid that he'd have to spend twice as long in the car with her, and by the time he arrived, the last bite of his mother's roast would have been eaten.

That would be terrible.

Of course, it wasn't the worst thing that could happen. The worst thing, God forbid, was that they couldn't make it home. Tasha wasn't thinking about that possibility—she'd always been an optimist—but he was already picturing them dead in a ditch, having slid off the icy road and down a cliff. Not that there were cliffs along any of his planned routes, but still.

His imagination was running away with itself. Most people probably thought Greg had a terrible imagination, but it was really quite active.

He took a few deep breaths, but with the noise in the car, it was impossible to calm himself down. The current song was "Holly Jolly Christmas," which he thought was incredibly stupid.

The next song was no better: "The Twelve Days of Christmas." Who would willingly listen to every verse of this song?

His ex-girlfriend, apparently. She was singing along and seemed to be enjoying herself.

Alas, she didn't have a good voice. It was unfortunate, given how much she enjoyed singing. She was smart and talented, skilled at many things, but this was not one of them, and her voice hadn't improved over time. He couldn't help a fond smile but quickly schooled his features into a frown.

"Can we please go back to CBC?" he asked.

"So you've become a CBC Radio junkie," she said. "Isn't their average listener, like, a sixty-five-year-old white man in a sweater vest?"

"It's informative. I learn lots of things by listening to the radio."

"Mm-hmm."

"What? I do."

Why, the other day he'd heard a fascinating twenty-minute segment about snails on *Quirks and Quarks*.

"I shouldn't be surprised," she said. "Listening to CBC Radio seems like the sort of thing you'd do. You were always a bit of an old man, even when you were sixteen."

He shrugged.

She didn't seem to intend it as an insult—Tasha wasn't a mean-spirited person—and there was lots of truth to it.

Just wait until she found out about his model railway.

"I have refined tastes," he said, lifting his nose in the air for effect.

She snort-laughed, and—against his will—his lips twitched.

They twitched again when she sang about maids a-milking, loud and out of tune. It hurt his eardrums, but it was kind of adorable and—

No! What was wrong with him? He didn't like this, not one bit.

Finally, the horrid song about turtle doves and swans a-swimming was finished, but the next song was even worse.

"All I Want for Christmas Is You."

He couldn't take it anymore.

"Shut that off," he said through clenched teeth.

"What's wrong, Mr. Grinch?"

"I don't like Christmas music."

"I seem to recall something to that effect."

Dammit, this woman drove him mad.

"Please?" she said. "You know I love Christmas music. Things have been so busy at work, and I haven't gotten to listen to it much this year."

"Fine. But not this song. Anything but 'All I Want for Christmas Is You.'"

All Greg wanted for Christmas was a little peace and quiet and some roast beef.

Not Tasha.

She skipped ahead to "Silent Night," which wasn't so awful. He still didn't like it, but it didn't make him grind his teeth.

"I remember now," Tasha said. "Why you hate Christmas music, especially that song."

He grunted.

She touched his shoulder. "I still have the necklace. I don't wear it anymore, but I never got rid of it."

In high school, Greg had worked in the summers—once pollinating corn, and once at the nearby provincial park—but he hadn't worked much during the school year, aside from a little tutoring.

Except for December of his final year of high school.

He'd gotten a seasonal job in Sarnia so he could buy Tasha something nice for Christmas. He'd hated every minute of that retail job. The worst part was that Christmas music was playing all the damn time, and every third song, for whatever reason, had been "All I Want for Christmas Is You."

He hadn't minded the song before that. He really hadn't. But when you were subjected to it every ten minutes during an eight-hour shift...well, it got to you. You started fantasizing about strangling Santa Claus and Rudolph and stuff like that.

But despite the temptation, he hadn't quit that job, and he'd saved up enough money to buy a necklace from The Bay, the one he'd had his eye on. She'd adored it—as he'd known she would—and he'd thought it was all worth it.

To be honest, he missed feeling like he would do anything for a woman because he loved her so much.

They'd been young, but he'd loved her.

It had been quite a while since he'd felt like that about anyone. Tasha, however, wasn't the solution to his lack of love life. They'd already been together, and it hadn't worked out.

Besides, despite some common interests, they were too different.

Case in point: he'd prefer to spend their road trip listening to CBC like an old fogey, and she'd prefer to play "The Twelve Days of Christmas" and sing off-tune at the top of her lungs.

And sure, he could admit that she looked nice in her sweater and had a lovely smile, but he refused to admit that her enthusiastic singing was even a little bit charming.

No, he would most certainly not do that.

Tasha sighed and reluctantly turned CBC Radio One back on, though she couldn't suppress a small smile as she recalled Greg's reaction to her singing "Deck the Halls."

He hadn't changed at all, and yet at the same time...he had.

As he focused on the road, she snuck a glance at him. There were fine lines at the corner of his eye—those hadn't been there before. Earlier, she'd noticed two lines between his eyebrows. His features were a little more angular, and now that they were in the car and he'd thrown his winter coat in the back seat, she could get a better look at the rest of him. He was definitely more solid than before. His bicep looked rather nice actually, and she wondered how it would feel if she wrapped her hand around it.

Stop it, Tasha!

Sure, she still found the man attractive. They'd dated for a long time; that was hardly surprising. But it was nothing more than that.

"Thank you again for driving me home," she said.

He grunted.

"It's really nice of you. I guess our moms ran into each other at the grocery store and—"

"Yeah, I know." His voice was clipped. "And my mom called me this morning and made a point of saying you're single. She's clearly hoping we'll get back together."

"What? No."

"Trust me. That's what she wants."

"But that's ridiculous," Tasha said. "First of all, I don't believe in second chances at relationships. Getting back together with an ex never turns out well. Second of all, we dated a *long* time ago. Fifteen years."

He grunted again. "Yes, I'm aware of that."

"I'm surprised you're not married, actually. I can imagine you cuddled up by the fireplace with a woman, each of you wearing a sweater vest and drinking a single glass of wine while you listen to CBC. Sensible presents wrapped under the Christmas tree. Maybe a French press or a fancy screwdriver. A model train if you feel really daring."

His gaze was focused on the road. "It might interest you to know that I have an elaborate model railway in my den."

She couldn't tell if he was joking. Greg's sense of humor did occasionally make an appearance. He'd say something ridiculous in such a calm voice that you'd believe it.

"Really, I do," he said. "I'll show you pictures and you can laugh at me."

She chuckled. Now that she thought of it, a model railway wasn't ridiculous at all. It fit him—and his detail-oriented brain—perfectly. She imagined this sweater-vest-wearing lady buying him tiny buildings and trees to go alongside the railway, and Greg being so overcome with love that he gave her a single peck on the cheek.

No. Greg hadn't been that restrained as a lover. He'd been passionate. Thorough.

Tasha's cheeks heated and she pushed those thoughts aside. She was probably misremembering a lot of things. After all, it had been many years.

For five minutes, she listened to someone on the radio talk about the weather, but dammit, she kept thinking of him kissing her, and that wouldn't do. They didn't suit each other, and sure he was handsome, but there were other handsome men, ones who grunted less and actually liked Christmas music. Crispin, for example.

Tasha always looked forward, never back. She tried not to think too much about the past, and Greg was firmly in her past. The only time she'd broken her own rule and given an ex a second chance, it had failed spectacularly. She'd seen it fail many times for her friends, too.

Nope, no matter what his mother thought, nothing was happening between them.

She let him enjoy the rest of the scintillating weather report, then put on "Wonderful Christmastime."

Greg's lips thinned, but he didn't speak.

"Come on, get in the spirit!" she said.

"You know me. 'Spirited' is the last thing anyone would say about me."

She suppressed a laugh.

She couldn't help wanting to needle him. She wouldn't play "All I Want for Christmas Is You," but she'd play all the other songs in her Christmas folder. And to annoy him further, she started singing along.

He mumbled something that sounded suspiciously like, "Damn infernal racket."

It was snowing quite a bit now—more than a snowflake here and there. Perhaps it would take five hours to get home rather than three, but that was okay. Greg might be a Grinch, but she was having a grand old time with her Christmas music, and once she got home, there would be hot chocolate with her parents in the living room, accompanied by the fragrance of the Christmas tree. Though she couldn't imagine living in Mosquito Bay—and not just because there were no jobs for aerospace engineers—she enjoyed going back to see her family. It was nice to have a small town to visit, away from the bustle of the city.

"Jingle Bell Rock" was next, and she sang along to that, too, until a memory popped into her brain.

She'd once stripped to this song for Greg.

They'd been in their first year of university, home for the holidays. Her parents had gone out for the day, so she'd taken advantage of that and asked Greg to come over. She'd only gotten about halfway through the song before she'd burst into laughter. He'd tackled her, and they'd laughed together before having sex on the floor.

Tasha couldn't listen to this song anymore.

She flipped to the next one: "Do They Know It's Christmas?"

"Yes, Goddammit," Greg said a minute later. "I know it's Christmas. I don't know how I could bloody forget it's Christmas, what with all the music I've had to endure on this trip." He shook his head. "Do you remember that movie with the green ogre? We watched it together once."

"Shrek. You two have a lot of similarities. The resemblance is rather uncanny."

He shot her a look. "You're like the sidekick in that movie. The donkey. The one who's very annoying."

"Gee, thanks. Why can't I be the princess instead?"

They'd been moving slowly, but now they came to a stop on the highway. They hadn't even gotten to Waterloo, and it felt like they'd been in the car for hours. It was already dark.

"People drive like idiots in the snow," he said. "If only you hadn't been late, we could have gotten out before the heavy traffic."

"I think the traffic would still have been bad if we left at three."

"Not as bad as it is now." He gestured to the windshield with one hand. "The snow wasn't supposed to start until later. Why couldn't the meteorologists have done a better job predicting this? Why couldn't the snow have waited until we were closer to Mosquito Bay? Dammit, I'm not sure we'll even get home tonight."

"You've sure spoken a lot in the past minute. What a novelty."

He didn't reply, just tightened his grip on the steering wheel.

"It'll be fine," she said.

"Nothing is going according to plan."

"When does life ever work that way? Don't worry, we'll get home tonight."

"Nick will have already eaten all my prime rib," Greg grumbled.

"Such a tragedy. Why do you have to be so negative?"

"I'm looking at the situation realistically."

Tasha turned off the music and let him listen to the radio in peace. She sent a text to her best friend, Monique. *My ex is annoying me. Trust me, there's no chance of us falling in love again.*

Thank God, Monique said. *But still. Be careful.*

Monique had been concerned when Tasha had told her that she was going back to Mosquito Bay with her high school boyfriend. Last year, Monique had hooked up with her boyfriend from grad school, and it had ended even worse than the first time. He'd promised he'd changed, but he hadn't.

I won't do anything stupid, Tasha said. *I promise.*

She closed her eyes for a few minutes and listened to the news.

And that's when she really started to worry.

The top news story was the snowstorm, which was packing much more heat—or, err, snow—than meteorologists had predicted earlier. The list of delays, road closures, and accidents was alarming. She checked Google Maps on her phone, and it was showing nearly their entire route in red.

Perhaps Greg had a point.

This wasn't simply driving back to Mosquito Bay in a little snow.

This could be bad.

And she was trapped in a car with her ex.

On the plus side, Greg had always been a careful driver. Though he might freak out, he was actually good at performing under stress and he prepared for everything.

So while the situation was less than ideal, and she didn't look forward to spending several more hours with him, she acknowledged that it could be worse.

She could be in a car with a different ex-boyfriend. Like Lance.

She shuddered at the thought.

"Cold?" Greg asked.

She shook her head. "I'm fine."

"Alright." He didn't sound convinced, but he let it go.

"...particularly bad near London and Strathroy," said the voice on the radio.

Great. That was exactly where they were heading. London, Ontario was about two hours from Toronto—on a normal day—and Mosquito Bay was to the northwest of it.

After sending her parents a quick text to let them know where she was and that she would be late, Tasha closed her eyes once more and leaned her head against the door. She tried to think of sugar plums and shortbread cookies.

It didn't work. Her mind kept coming up with pictures of blizzards instead.

Chapter 3

IT'S GOING TO BE okay. It's going to be okay.

Greg took a deep breath and repeated the words to himself again.

It's going to be okay.

Sure, he could barely see two meters in front of the car, and the wipers were swishing frantically across the windshield, but they were still slowly moving, and there weren't near as many cars on the road out here. Most people were sensible enough to stay off the roads.

If only he'd done the same.

But he'd been convinced they could outrun the storm. Nobody had predicted it would be this bad.

And if Tasha hadn't been late...

He should stop fixating on that. It might not have made a huge difference in this weather.

He grabbed a protein bar from the console and had a bite. He would offer one to Tasha, but she'd been asleep for the past hour.

Good.

He didn't need to listen to more horrific Christmas music, or hear her chatter when there wasn't much to say.

Well, he supposed there was a lot to say. A lot had happened in the past fifteen years. But what was the point of catching up with someone who wasn't going to stay in your life?

Better that she sleep so he could concentrate on the road.

Though she did look quite pretty. She'd put on a white toque, and her braids peeked out from the bottom. Her eyelashes fluttered against her dark cheeks.

Yes, he'd glanced at her once or twice before quickly turning back to the snowy road.

And then she snored.

It brought a smile to his lips.

He quickly wiped it away. What the hell was wrong with him?

Despite all the years that had passed, apparently he'd retained a strange affection for her snores. She'd never snored a lot, but on one occasion, it had woken him up, and then he'd watched her sleep in his arms.

There was definitely something wrong with him. Perhaps he needed some caffeine. As a general rule, he didn't drink coffee after six o'clock in the evening, but this was going to be a long night, and he didn't want to fall asleep at the wheel.

Though with all the adrenaline coursing through his veins, there probably wasn't much danger of that, but coffee would make this terrible drive more pleasant.

He continued forward at a slow pace. They had exited the 401 and were now on the 402. Normally, this would be an hour or less from Mosquito Bay, but in a snowstorm, it was anyone's guess. It could be hours from here. He'd switched from CBC to an all-news channel.

"…closed just west of Strathroy…"

Dammit! Was the 402 closed west of Strathroy? That wouldn't be surprising, not in these conditions. But the radio was on low, so as not to disturb Tasha, and he hadn't heard clearly.

He turned up the volume, and a few minutes later, the radio host repeated the closure.

It was indeed the 402.

Greg blew out a breath.

It's going to be okay. It's going to be okay.

But he'd have to take the next exit. He could try driving on back roads to Mosquito Bay, but that probably wouldn't be a good idea. Mosquito Bay was still a ways away, and those roads were likely in poor condition. And it was dark.

He glanced over at Tasha again.

He didn't want anything to happen to her.

They should stop for the night. If he remembered correctly, there was a little motel only a kilometer or so from the next exit. He could get them each a room. Not ideal, but it was for the best.

He blew out another breath as he got off the highway and made his way north. He was starting to worry he'd been wrong about that motel when the orange neon letters came into view: Sugar Maple Motel.

It looked like it had been built fifty years ago and not updated since. Still, better than sleeping in the car.

His heart was thumping too quickly. He was supposed to be in Mosquito Bay tonight, eating dinner with his family. They were too loud and they drove him mad, but he loved them anyway.

Except now he was stopping at a motel for the night with Tasha, a situation he had not prepared for at *all*.

A week of mental preparation for this would have been nice. Better yet, a month.

He tapped her shoulder. She mumbled something inarticulate, her eyes still closed, so he did it again.

"Are we there?" she asked.

"No, the 402 is closed. We'll have to stay at a motel for the night."

She was wide awake now. A range of emotions passed over her face, and then she pressed her lips together. "Okay."

He was already forming new plans in his mind. Hopefully there was food at the motel, but there probably wouldn't be much. However, he had water, protein bars, and snacks in his trunk, so they'd be okay. Tasha might want to hang out for a little while and talk, and he supposed he could put up with that. Then they could head to their separate rooms by ten o'clock. He'd do some reading and go to bed well before midnight; she'd probably listen to some more Christmas music. There was no point trying to get up early tomorrow, since it would take a while to plow the roads, but Greg would get on the road by mid-morning and be home by lunch.

Yep, that was his new plan.

Oh, and he'd have to text his family to inform them of this unfortunate delay.

He pulled his down jacket tightly around him to protect himself from the brutal wind, then headed to the motel, Tasha behind him. When he opened the door to the motel office, chimes tinkled above the door.

"I'm so sorry," said the woman behind the desk. According to her nametag, her name was Clara. She was white, a little younger than his own mother, her brown hair heavily streaked with gray. "We're full."

Oh, no.

Lots of people must have already stopped here due to the storm. His new plan was crumbling before his eyes.

"Are you sure?" Greg croaked. "There's nothing at all?"

Clara hesitated. "Well, we do have one room."

"Great, we'll take it."

"But the heat stopped working earlier in the day, and the repairman won't be here to fix it until tomorrow. I'll give it to you for half price."

When they'd set out on their road trip five hours ago, this was not where Greg had expected to end up. In a crappy motel, thankful there was one room available, even if it had no heat.

"That's fine," Tasha said. "We can manage."

"It's nasty out there tonight, eh?" Clara asked as she pulled out the key for their room. Yes, this motel had actual keys, not key cards. "Terrible storm. Poor Bobby is trembling in fright." She gestured to a Shih Tzu, lying on the thin carpet.

In Greg's opinion, "Bobby" was a terrible name for a dog.

A few minutes later, they hauled their suitcases to the door of their room, the wind whipping the snow around them. It really was unpleasant out here.

Some part of Greg's brain—the highly delusional part—was thrilled with this situation. He'd get to spend the night in the same room as Tasha, who sure did look cute all bundled up. He pictured her undressing, sliding her hand down his body. They'd had a lot of fun together, back in the day...

Nope, not happening. His imagination needed to calm the fuck down.

He put the key into the lock and turned. The door opened, and he flicked on the lights. It wasn't warm in here, but at least there was no wind.

However, there was only one bed.

Chapter 4

TASHA RUBBED HER EYES and looked again.

No, her eyes hadn't been deceiving her. There really was only one bed.

Once upon a time, this would have been a luxury for them. A night alone together in a motel room with a queen-size bed? Even without any heat, that would have been exciting.

They'd spent some nights together in university, but not a ton, and it required sharing a twin bed, which hadn't exactly been comfortable since Greg wasn't a small guy.

Yep, eighteen-year-old Tasha would have *loved* this situation.

But now, a queen bed wasn't a luxury to her—she had one at home—and Greg wasn't her boyfriend. Now, a queen bed didn't seem big enough.

She looked over at Greg. The look of horror on his face nearly made her laugh.

She wasn't looking forward to spending the night in a motel with him. He wouldn't want to listen to Christmas music or even talk. He'd probably just grunt and scowl a lot.

But although she hadn't spoken to Greg much in years, she trusted him, and he'd gotten them there safely, and eventually they'd make it to Mosquito Bay. Sure, he could be irritating at times, but he wasn't a bad guy.

She'd have to make the best of it. That's what she always did.

She marched into the room and took off her boots and winter jacket, which she hung in the small closet. She didn't remove her toque or her big sweater—thank God she was dressed for this weather—and climbed into bed.

"Aren't you coming?" she asked Greg, who was still standing by the door.

"I...I just..."

It was kind of cute to see him stammer.

"I don't bite," she said. "I promise."

He didn't look convinced, just stood there in brooding silence.

"There's only one bed!" he blurted out at last.

Her lips twitched. "Yes, I'm aware, but it's a big bed. Don't worry, you won't catch any Christmas spirit from me."

"I like Christmas. I just don't like Christmas music."

"*Jingle bells, jingle bells...*" she began singing.

He visibly shuddered.

"Don't worry," she said. "I won't do any more singing tonight." But she hadn't been able to resist teasing him one last time.

"Thank God," he muttered.

"Instead, we'll have a long, heart-to-heart conversation until two in the morning."

He looked equally horrified by that prospect.

They would have enjoyed that sort of thing when they were younger, though. Sure, she would have done three-quarters of the talking, but he'd have been a willing participant.

"Just kidding," she said. "I'm going to call my mom and tell her where we are."

He nodded before coming to sit beside her on the bed. The mattress dipped under his weight, and she exhaled unsteadily. This was how close he'd be to her, all night.

He must have noticed her response, because he said, "I could sit at the table until bedtime, if you prefer." He gestured to the crappy wooden table and two chairs by the window.

"No, stay here. It's more comfortable."

He grunted in acknowledgement.

She set her purse on the night-table and fished out her phone. *Shit.* She'd missed two calls from her parents while she was sleeping and sorting out the motel situation. She immediately gave them a call.

"Tasha!" her mother said. "Where are you?"

"I'm sorry. You were probably worried sick. We're in a motel near Strathroy. We won't make it home tonight."

It ached to say those words. She'd resolved to make the best of this, but she really wished she was at home with her parents, cuddled up under a blanket while watching a movie and drinking hot chocolate.

She should try to make it home more often. She loved living in Toronto and wouldn't have it any other way, but the downside was that she was far from her parents, and they were getting old. Tasha's parents had had her later in life; they were a good ten years older than Greg's parents.

She'd wanted to have children earlier than her mom had, but she was now thirty-four and single.

She took a few deep breaths. No, she wouldn't let this get her down. A new year was starting soon—a new year of opportunities. She had a good career, the one she'd dreamed of since high school, and a condo. Her car had died, but she would get another one soon. She wasn't rich, but she was comfortable. She had a decent life, and she had to believe the right man would come around soon. There was always hope.

And maybe she'd already met the right man. She'd gone on a few dates with Crispin, and they'd been pleasant enough. Perhaps it would just take time for her to feel that spark.

"Thank God," her mother said. "It's quite the storm out there."

"Unfortunately, there's no heat in our room." Tasha wrapped one arm around herself and pulled her toque lower on her ears. "And we—"

"Wait a second. You said 'our room.'"

"We have to share a room because it's the last one, and it only has one bed. But it's okay. Nothing we haven't done before, right?"

Greg got up and headed outside, presumably to get something from his car.

On the other end of the phone, her mom was laughing. "It's a sign!"

"No, Mom, it's not a *sign*."

Her mother was still laughing. She was such a romantic.

Though she hadn't been thrilled when Tasha and Greg had started dating in grade eleven. She hadn't wanted anything to get in the way of Tasha pursuing her dreams.

But Greg, who'd always seemed older than his years, had won her over. He was not the kind of guy who got a girl into trouble or discouraged her ambitions, as her mother's first husband had done.

And now that Tasha had an established career and was over thirty, her mother kept talking about signs and romance all the time.

Which was fine.

But Greg was her ex-boyfriend, and Tasha always looked forward, never back.

"I always liked him," Mom said.

"No, you didn't. You thought he'd distract me."

"Silly of me. I should have known my girl would never get distracted."

Tasha couldn't help but smile.

"It's so cold outside, and when you're huddled up under the covers together, who knows what will happen?"

"Mom!" Tasha wasn't smiling now.

"Rosemary was clearly hoping that you and Greg would get back together when she suggested he drive you home for the holidays. I wasn't thinking of that, just thought it would be convenient for you, but now—"

"Alright, Mom. Enough with the matchmaking. Nothing is going to happen between us."

"You say that, but—"

"Mom!"

"Okay, okay, I'll stop," Mom said. "Guess what I made? Gingerbread cookies."

Tasha's tummy rumbled. She hadn't eaten dinner yet. In fact, she hadn't eaten in nearly nine hours. Hot chocolate and gingerbread sounded delicious.

They talked for a few more minutes, and as soon as Tasha set down her phone on the table next to the bed, a mug of hot chocolate appeared beside it.

She rubbed her eyes. She must be hallucinating. Or she'd gained special powers and had conjured up the hot chocolate just by thinking about it.

That would be a useful skill, but it seemed unlikely.

No, she must be hallucinating.

She reached for the mug, just in case.

It was real. Totally real. She had a sip, and though it was fairly ordinary hot chocolate, it was especially good because she was freezing right now. It warmed her from the inside.

"Figured you could use something hot," Greg said.

She whipped her head around. He was sitting in bed next to her, his legs crossed at the ankles. His glasses were on his night-table, next to a steaming mug, though it looked like he was drinking tea, not hot chocolate. He'd always been a big tea drinker. She used to tease him about it.

"It's delicious." She looked around the room and saw an electric kettle on the table, which she could have sworn wasn't there before. "Where did that come from?"

He chuckled, a soft sound that made her smile. "I had the kettle, mugs, tea, and hot chocolate in my car."

"Why?"

He shrugged. "Part of my winter survival kit. Plus, it's useful to have a kettle in my bedroom when I visit Mom and Dad, so I don't have to talk to anyone if I want tea. Going down to the kitchen is an arduous affair."

She couldn't help but laugh, though she was still wrapping her mind around the fact that he traveled with all those things. "What else do you have in your car?"

He gestured toward the chairs. There were two sleeping bags, an extra blanket, a couple hats and gloves, and... Oh My God.

"A space heater!" She could kiss him.

She covered her mouth and looked away. She shouldn't be thinking like that. This was Greg Wong, after all.

And this was such a *Greg* thing to do. To be prepared for the unlikely event of staying in a motel with no heat.

"You have any food in your car?" she asked.

He held out three bars: a granola bar, a protein bar, and a Coffee Crisp. "Appetizer, main course, and dessert."

She'd never been so happy to see a granola bar in her life. And a Coffee Crisp!

"You travel with Coffee Crisps in your car?" she asked, gesturing to the yellow wrapper of the chocolate bar. These were her favorite, but not his.

He shook his head. "There's a vending machine in the motel office."

Oh. He'd gotten it just for her. Because he remembered.

This, too, was such a Greg thing. He'd always quietly looked after her in little ways.

"Do you have food for yourself?" she asked, suddenly worried he'd given it all to her.

"I ate a protein bar while you were sleeping in the car, but I have more, don't worry." He held up a granola bar and some trail mix. "You talked to your mother?"

"Yeah, I assured her that I'm perfectly fine and not freezing to death in a snowstorm. Did you talk to your family?"

"I texted my brother." He cocked his head in the direction of his phone.

Greg *texted*. It seemed all wrong.

To her, Greg was the past. When they'd been together, neither of them had a smartphone. Texting wasn't really a thing yet.

"Remember how much time we used to spend on MSN Messenger?" she asked.

He smiled faintly. "I do."

Back when they were at different universities, it was the main way they'd stayed in contact. Daily conversations on MSN Messenger before they went to bed. Weekends together maybe once a month. Toronto and Waterloo weren't all that far apart, but there was always so much schoolwork to do, so much going on, and it had been hard to see each other.

"I'm going to get changed," she said.

She dug around in her suitcase, then went to the washroom to take off her bra and change into her flannel pajama pants. She looked in the mirror afterward and found herself wanting to touch up her make-up.

Stop it, Tasha. It's just Greg.

Yes, they were sharing a bed in a snowstorm, but tomorrow they would go back to their regularly scheduled lives, without each other.

And that was fine. It was what she wanted.

She texted Monique again, telling her that they'd had to stop at a motel, but Tasha emphasized, once again, that there was no danger of her falling in love.

She didn't mention the Coffee Crisp or the hot chocolate, though.

Chapter 5

When Tasha came out of the washroom, she was still wearing the same cream-colored sweater, but she had plaid pajama pants on now.

It was the opposite of revealing, but Greg's jeans suddenly felt a little tight.

He should not be lusting after Tasha, but he couldn't help being attracted to her, even all these years later.

They'd been in the same class throughout elementary school. There was only one class per grade in Mosquito Bay, and he was the only Asian kid and she was the only Black kid in their year. He hadn't talked to her—or anyone else—much, preferring to sit in the corner and work in silence. He'd been a very serious child.

High school was bigger than elementary school, since kids from a few of the nearby towns were bussed to Mosquito Bay. He'd spent much of grade ten math admiring her from the back corner, and in grade eleven, they'd been in physics together. When they'd had to do their first ticker tape lab, she'd turned to him and asked with a bright smile if he'd be her lab partner. He'd smiled and croaked out a "yes," already half in love with her.

She had smooth brown skin and a lovely smile. Nice ass, maybe a little bigger now—and he wasn't complaining.

Stop it, Greg.

He should not be looking at her ass.

They were just sharing a bed, nothing more.

She climbed under the covers, and he went to the washroom to change into his pajamas. When he returned, she was chewing on her protein bar—and his gaze immediately latched onto her lips.

He turned away and picked up his e-reader. Hopefully, she would get the point and realize he didn't want to talk.

For half an hour, he read and she did something on her phone. Although he couldn't forget that she was sitting next to him in bed, it was still comfortable, somehow.

"We never did this before," he said, surprising himself by talking. It was rare for him to break the silence. Tasha was the talkative one, but she'd respected his need for quiet for the thirty minutes, which he appreciated.

"Did what, you mean?"

"Sit quietly in bed together. Whenever there was a bed..." He trailed off, his cheeks heating.

"Please, continue." She smirked.

"We were all over each other," he said hoarsely.

The silence now was distinctly *un*comfortable. She seemed to be checking him out, or was that his imagination? Surely Tasha had better options than him, even if she was single at the moment.

But for a few seconds, he allowed himself to recall what it had been like to be a horny teenager rolling around in bed with her.

"We only ever had a twin bed," he said. "A queen, even in a cheap motel without heat, would have been a luxury."

"That's exactly what I thought when we stepped inside the room."

"Sharing a queen-size bed? Piece of cake." He made a dismissive gesture with his hand.

This, of course was a lie. He was very much aware of how close she was. It would be so easy to reach out and touch her.

He wouldn't.

"We could have rolled over to change positions without toppling onto the floor," Tasha said. "Definitely a luxury."

They were both quiet again. He was thinking about all the sex they'd had, and he wondered if she was thinking about that, too. He wouldn't flatter himself and assume she was. She'd probably had much better sex in the intervening years.

After all, they'd been each other's firsts. First *everything*. It had been a year before they'd had sex—over Christmas holidays when they were both seventeen—but there had been an awful lot of fooling around before that, whenever they had a chance to be alone.

They wouldn't have wasted an opportunity like this one.

"Why did you ask me to be your lab partner?" he asked suddenly.

"You were smart, and I wanted a good mark without having to do all the work myself."

"Mm." He set aside his book, figuring he wouldn't get much more reading done tonight, and he was okay with that.

"And I was right. We had the two highest marks in the class."

She'd beaten him by a couple percent in grade eleven physics, but he'd gotten the higher mark in grade twelve.

"I can't believe I worked up the nerve to ask you on a date," he said. "I'd wanted to do it for months before I finally managed to get the words out."

"You stuttered. Do you remember that?"

"I most certainly did not stutter."

"You did! It was cute."

"I don't think 'cute' was quite what I was going for, and I doubt anyone has described me as cute in decades."

She laughed. "You sound so offended by the thought."

He responded with an exaggerated sniff.

Which made her laugh again.

Greg knew he wasn't a particularly funny guy. He was positive everyone thought he was less funny than his brothers. But he'd always been able to make Tasha laugh—rarely a belly-aching laugh, but a quiet chuckle. He was glad he could still do so.

She tore open the wrapper of the Coffee Crisp and took a big bite. He was pleased he'd been able to get one at the poorly-stocked vending machine in the motel. Personally, Greg didn't much care for candy bars—they were overly sweet and terrible for you. He wasn't a huge dessert person in general, although there were a few things he liked.

But in grade twelve, she'd told him her locker combo, and he never used it unless she specifically asked him to grab something for her, except for the handful of times he'd snuck in to put a Coffee Crisp and a note on the top shelf in her locker.

She'd always rewarded him with a big kiss afterward.

Geez, it had been a long time since he'd thought of these things. So strange to be in bed with her after all this time.

"Is Coffee Crisp still your favorite?" he asked.

"Yeah, but I don't have them much anymore. Haven't had one in months, actually."

Just then, the wind howled outside, and Tasha shivered. Before he knew what he was doing, his arms were around her. It felt good to hold her again.

And then he realized what he was doing and immediately sat back.

"Sorry," he mumbled.

"You scared of the wind?" she teased.

"No, I'm not scared of a little winter weather."

"You built me that snow fort, remember? So we could have a place to be alone together."

He'd certainly not forgotten about that.

They'd only gotten to spend a couple weekends together in their first term of university. Having two and a half weeks back in Mosquito Bay for the holidays seemed like heaven.

Except their families were *always* home, and the cars were often in use.

Then there had been a big snowfall, and he'd done a little research online about making structurally-stable snow forts. He'd built quite an elaborate one, though he didn't put a roof on it, afraid it would collapse—he used a tarp instead. And then he'd brought her to the park at the edge of town, asked her to close her eyes, and led her inside.

She'd been delighted.

For three days, they'd spent a lot of time in the snow fort. They could make out in peace and quiet, and he'd bring a big thermos of tea to keep them warm. But then a bunch of kids had knocked it down.

It was a pleasant memory, as were most of his memories of their time together. They had completely opposite personalities, but they'd fit together well, and when she got on his nerves, he'd still felt an annoyed affection for her. He just hadn't let himself reminisce in a long time, because after their break-up, it had been too painful.

Their relationship had gone out with a whimper, not a bang. No big fight. Neither of them had met someone else.

But it was hard to maintain a relationship when you were going to university in different cities.

When they were in their final year of high school, she'd dreamed of studying engineering science at U of T, with the plan of specializing in aerospace engineering in third year, and he'd hoped to do systems engineering at Waterloo, which was known for its co-op program.

They'd both gotten into the programs they wanted, and they'd talked about it a lot, but neither of them had felt like the other person should make sacrifices so they could be together. Conventional wisdom said you shouldn't make your decision about university based on where your boyfriend or girlfriend was going.

So they hadn't.

Many people also said you shouldn't marry your high school sweetheart.

Greg's parents had started dating in high school, though, and secretly, he'd thought he and Tasha would end up together, like his parents. Sure, he constantly heard about how these strong emotions were just a teenage thing, blah, blah, blah, but he hadn't believed that.

"No other man has ever built me a snow fort," Tasha said.

"Or gotten you stranded in a crappy motel near Strathroy."

"You're not blaming that on me being twenty-seven minutes late?"

He shrugged. If he was honest with himself, he didn't actually mind being trapped in a motel room with Tasha Edwards, much to his surprise.

"Do you like living in Toronto?" she asked. "I do. It's all that I wanted it to be, and it's hard for me to imagine living in a small town now."

"I like it. I plan to stay." He'd first started thinking about moving to Toronto back when he and Tasha were together—he thought he'd go to school in Waterloo, then move to Toronto with her, since she'd always dreamed of living in the big city. Once he graduated, there was no girlfriend in the picture, but he got an offer for a decent job in Toronto, and so he stuck with that part of his plan. He'd been there for over a decade now, and it was hard for him to imagine living elsewhere, too.

His phone rang, and he picked it up.

"Greg!" said a loud voice.

"Hi, Ah Ma."

"You kiss yet?"

Well, his grandmother had certainly gotten straight to the point.

He scrubbed a hand over his face and glanced over at Tasha. He imagined putting his arms around her again and—

"No," he said curtly, very much aware that Tasha could hear anything he said. She was texting now, a slight smile on her lips.

"You are sharing a room, I hope?" Ah Ma asked.

It was so weird. When you were a teenager, your parents and grandparents were always trying to prevent you from having a little alone time with your girlfriend. When you were thirty-four and they feared you'd never get married, they were desperately trying to throw you together with your ex.

"Yes," he said.

"There is only one bed? When I read romance books, this is what always happens."

"Yes."

She cackled, then turned away from the phone and said loudly, "They have to share a bed!"

Great. Now everyone in his family would know his business.

There was silence on the other end of the phone for the moment, and then a male voice spoke. "You need any advice on how to make a move?"

It was Nick, who was two years younger than Greg, and, admittedly, much more well-versed in the art of seduction.

But Greg did not need advice from his brother, and he was not trying to seduce Tasha.

"Mind your own business," he snapped.

Tasha chuckled. Her face was framed by her long braids, and God, why was that toque with the pom-pom so cute on her?

"You still like her?" Nick asked.

Greg grunted.

"I'll take that to mean, 'Yes, absolutely, I want to jump her bones.'"

"Stop being so crude."

"You definitely want her."

"Nick..."

There was a pause on the other end of the phone before another voice said, "I ate all of your prime rib. Mm, was it ever good."

That was Zach.

Annoying little brothers. Why did Greg have two of them? And why did everyone in his family feel the need to speak to him on the phone so they could make more or less the same comments? It was a waste of time when he could be...well, not kissing Tasha, but quietly reading next to her or having a pleasant conversation. Preferable to dealing with his family.

His stomach rumbled at the thought of that prime rib. That granola bar hadn't been nearly as satisfying.

"Tell Tasha I say hi." Zach spoke in a singsong voice, clearly amused by the situation.

This was another comment that was best responded to with a grunt.

"You know, women like when you talk to them," Zach said.

"My specialty is listening," Greg said.

"And grunting."

"Grunting is very useful. It expresses a wide range of emotions."

Next to him, Tasha doubled over in laughter.

"Do you grunt a lot when you have sex?" Zach asked.

"I am not talking about my sex life with you," Greg replied.

Tasha's cheeks looked a little flushed now. He imagined her underneath him...

No, not happening.

"Okay, okay," Zach said. "I'll be good."

"Yeah, right," Greg muttered.

"Lily made Nanaimo bars and Mom made cheesecake, but it's all gone now."

Truth be told, Greg didn't particularly like Nanaimo bars, but he wanted some damn cheesecake. It was his favorite dessert. His mom had given him the recipe, but his never turned out quite as good. Besides, what was the point of making a whole cheesecake when you lived alone? He didn't need that much cheesecake.

"Thanks for making me hungry," he said.

"You're welcome," Zach said cheerfully. "Anytime. Dad wants to talk to you now."

Their father's voice came over the phone. "Glad you're safe. It looks nasty out there."

"It is," Greg said.

"You know, the cheesecake was *really* good."

Okay, that was enough. "I'm getting off the phone now. See you tomorrow."

Greg ended the call and shook his head.

"'Grunting is very useful and expresses a wide range of emotions,'" Tasha said in a fake deep voice.

"Thank you." He kept his expression stern, but admittedly, he enjoyed when she teased him.

She looked down at her phone.

"What are you doing now?" he asked.

"Talking to the guy I'm seeing."

He couldn't help the jealousy that coursed through him, but he shouldn't be jealous. Sure, he could appreciate that Tasha was a good-looking woman, and he still liked spending time with her, but that was all. She wasn't *his*; she could date whomever she liked.

"We've just been on a couple dates," she said. "Nothing serious. He's not my boyfriend, and we're not spending the holidays together. But he's a good guy."

Unsure what to say but feeling he should acknowledge her words, Greg grunted.

See? It really was a useful sound.

"You seeing anyone?" she asked, putting aside her phone.

"Nah," he said. "Not for a while now."

"Oh." She paused, looking thoughtful. "Are you—"

Before she could finish her question, the lights went out.

Chapter 6

Tasha tried the lamp next to the bed.

Nope, nothing. As expected.

She couldn't help it. She burst into laughter.

The situation was so ridiculous. She was sitting in bed with her high school boyfriend, whom she'd hardly seen in fifteen years, as a snowstorm raged outside. There was no heat, and now, no power.

Across the bed, Greg's laughter rumbled, causing a pleasant vibration in her chest.

"You okay?" he asked.

"Yeah," she said. "I'm fine, though I guess the space heater won't do much for us now."

"Do you want one of the sleeping bags or the extra blanket?"

"Actually, yeah. The extra blanket would be good."

The mattress shifted as Greg got up. Soon, it dipped again as he climbed back in bed, and in the dark, she was acutely aware of his nearness.

For some reason, it felt like the sleepovers she'd gone to in elementary school. The lights were out, and they could giggle and talk about their secrets.

He placed the blanket over her, and she pulled it up to her neck.

"So, you haven't dated in a while," she said, returning to their conversation. "Like I told you, I'm surprised you're not married. You're the sort of man that a woman would settle down with—stable, kind, good job—versus the kind of man she'd have a hot fling with when she's young."

"You dated me when we were young."

Oh. She realized how it had sounded. "Not that we didn't have fun together. Not that the sex wasn't good. You're just husband material. I mean it as a compliment."

"I know."

She could hear the smile in his voice.

"So tell me." She was suddenly quite curious. "How many relationships have you had since we broke up?"

"Three. All lasted more than a year."

That sounded like Greg. He wasn't the kind of guy who'd bounce from one woman to another, and he wasn't scared of commitment.

"None of them were quite right, though," he said. "They didn't last as long as we did. And I'm terrible at meeting women. That involves, you know, socializing." He made a sound of displeasure. "I know that, since I'd like a relationship, I should put myself out there, but I'm not great at it. And online dating…"

"What's wrong with it? That way, you don't actually have to speak to someone right away. Just swipe right and send a message."

"I feel like I don't understand the social conventions. I tried, but very few women contacted me or replied to my messages, the rare times I sent them. Perhaps my profiles could have used some work."

"Ooh, I could help you with that!"

"Get in line," he said. "Nick, Zach, Amber, and Ah Ma have already offered their assistance."

"I'm not sure you should be taking online dating advice from your grandma."

"My thoughts exactly."

"How old are your grandparents? My mom sees them about town on occasion."

"Eighty-eight and eighty-nine."

She looked away for a moment, though she couldn't see him in the dark anyway. Her grandparents would be over ninety if they were still alive. She missed them.

Greg's hand settled on her shoulder, just for a second, before he withdrew. "I listed my interests as CBC Radio, model trains, birdwatching, stamp-collecting, and documentaries."

She couldn't suppress a fond smile. It was so *Greg*.

"You should have added 'baking.' That would interest some women." He'd baked for her a bunch of times. Chocolate chip cookies and other things. All delicious.

"I'll keep it under consideration. But online dating made me nervous and uncomfortable, so I let myself take a break. And most women our age seem to be in a relationship."

Except her.

"Someday, though," he said, "I'll try again."

She could hear the yearning in his voice. When they were younger, he'd talked of getting married and having a small family. She knew it was still what he wanted; Greg wasn't someone who changed his mind about such things.

He wouldn't want four children like his parents had, but he'd want one or two. They'd drive him crazy and mess up his ordered life, something she knew he secretly enjoyed.

There was a pang in her heart. She still cared for him, and she wanted him to have everything he desired.

She pictured them in the kitchen together, making cookies for their two small children, then shook her head.

He was part of her past, not her future.

When she got sad about her dating life, she reminded herself that tomorrow was another day, and sure, her biological clock was ticking, but she still had a little time.

That was how she kept her spirits up, kept putting herself out there again and again.

Always forward, never back.

Why, there was already a nice man who liked her.

"Perhaps," Greg mused, "the problem is that I never ask women to come upstairs and see my model trains."

"Like asking a lady to come upstairs and see your etchings."

"Precisely. Or 'Netflix and chill.'"

She laughed, imagining him asking a woman, very seriously, to watch Netflix and chill.

"So, model trains, eh?" she said, finding that rather adorable for some reason. "You spend your free time listening to CBC, painting little trees and figurines, and watching your little train chugging through your model mountain?"

"How did you know there was a mountain?"

"Oh, I just do."

Because she still knew him.

Sure, he had a proper job now and he'd gotten some new hobbies, but fundamentally, he was the same.

If he asked her to come up to see his model train, she'd probably say yes, and he'd undress her with extreme care...and afterward, he really would show her the model train.

"What about you?" he asked. "I thought you'd be married by now, too."

"Why did you think that?"

He made some inarticulate noises, then said, "You're smart and beautiful. Then and now." He spoke as though it was an indisputable fact.

She hesitated. "I wish it had happened, but it didn't. Sometimes, I feel like it's greedy to want a career *and* a family—"

"Nobody tells men that they can't have it all, and we get praised when we take our own kids to the park. You can want it all, too."

"I want what my parents have."

"Me, too." He paused. "This guy you were texting—did you meet him online?"

"Yeah. He was the first guy who hadn't opened with a dick pic in a depressingly long time. His name is Crispin."

Perhaps she shouldn't have told Greg that. It felt weird.

Crispin was an outgoing man who worked in sales. They'd had fun on their dates, and the kissing had been good, but they hadn't gone any further. She'd texted him earlier, after Greg had given her hot chocolate and a Coffee Crisp, to remind herself that she had other options. Maybe Crispin could be the one, or...

"Maybe I have unrealistic expectations when it comes to dating," she said.

"Expecting men not to send you unsolicited dick pics is very reasonable."

It was weird to hear "dick pic" in Greg's sensible voice.

"It's much more than that. I want to just *know*."

"I understand."

When he was on the phone with his family, he'd said his specialty was listening—in response to what, she wasn't quite sure.

But, yeah, he was a good listener. You always felt like he was giving you his undivided attention, seriously considering whatever you said, no matter how trivial or silly. And while he liked when things made sense logically, he accepted that not everything worked that way.

He'd told her once that half the reason he loved her was because she was pretty and smart and fun...and many other adjectives. The other half, he didn't think he'd ever be able to explain. It simply was.

Not knowing what to say now, she asked, "Do you really birdwatch?"

He didn't question the change in topic. "Yeah."

"I don't think I'd have the patience."

"That's fair."

They were quiet for a moment in the darkness of their cold hotel room, and then there was a very loud squeak next door, followed by more squeaks in a slow, steady rhythm.

·❤·❤·❤·❤·❤·

The people in the next room were having sex. Greg was certain of it.

And here, on the other side of the wall, he and Tasha were having a conversation in bed in the dark, and it couldn't help feeling intimate.

He couldn't deny it: he wanted to make the bed springs squeak with Tasha, too. Not just because it had been a long time since he'd had sex, but because it was *her*.

The bed springs next door continued to squeak. Tasha laughed, and Greg joined her.

"Why did we break up?" he asked suddenly.

"We were drifting apart. It was hard to maintain a relationship when we went to different schools."

He knew that, but he'd wanted to hear her answer. "What if I'd gone to U of T with you?"

"I couldn't have asked you to do that. You wanted the co-op program, and you wanted systems engineering."

"And I couldn't have asked you to give up what you wanted, either. But what if—"

"Greg," she said. "Don't."

"Maybe we should have tried harder."

But they'd been in university, and that had been their priority. Focusing on school had seemed like the right thing to do.

And he'd felt like he was a yoke around her neck, preventing her from fully enjoying the university experience. The high school boyfriend who'd outstayed his welcome, even if they still cared for each other. She should be meeting other guys, having lots of new experiences, not spending her limited free time talking to him on MSN Messenger. In the end, he'd been the one to suggest breaking up, but it had been mutual. They'd both agreed it wasn't working.

Perhaps it wouldn't have turned out any differently if they'd gone to the same university.

Squeak, squeak, squeak.

"*Oh, Ethel,*" said a muffled male voice.

Tasha laughed. "Ethel isn't a name you hear much anymore, is it?"

"It was my great-grandmother's name," Greg said.

"Can you imagine giving a little girl that name?"

"Many old names have become popular again."

"Yeah, but not 'Ethel.' Or 'Bertha.'"

"This is true."

"*Herbert!*" said a not-so-muffled female voice from the other side of the wall.

So the people next door were Ethel and Herbert. Charming.

"How old do you think they are?" Tasha asked.

"I bet they're two sixteen-year-olds who snuck off during the snowstorm."

"Ethel and Herbert, the coolest kids in school."

"No, with names like those, they're probably in their eighties. Perhaps they were heading out to visit their adult children for the holidays, and they stopped when the weather took a turn for the worse and decided to make the best of the power outage."

"I hope I'm still having sex when I'm eighty-five."

"Same here," he said. "I just hope I'm not so loud about it."

"I don't think there's much danger of that. You were never loud."

For half a minute, all he could hear was the squeak of the bed springs and his own breathing.

And then another, "*Oh, Herbert!*"

Greg felt a strange fondness for this older couple having sex in a dark motel room, though he wished they'd do it a little more quietly.

He also couldn't help wishing that he and Tasha hadn't drifted apart. Maybe they could be stuck in this motel as a married couple, with a small child sleeping between them.

He shouldn't think about it, but he did.

What if...

"Ethel!"

"Oh, Herbie!"

The squeaking got even louder, and Greg was more uncomfortable than amused, though he was also thinking about doing exactly the same thing with Tasha.

What would it be like to sleep with her now? Would it be as good as he remembered?

Was his memory faulty?

"Yes, just like that. Herbieeeee."

This was followed by a few bangs.

Dear God.

On the other side of the bed, Tasha chuckled, low and husky. Goddammit, he wanted her.

"I hope nobody busts their hip," she said.

"I hope they stop this infernal racket soon," he muttered.

She shifted toward him and put her hand on his shoulder. "You sound like an old man." But she said it with affection, and he didn't mind at all.

Tentatively, he reached out and ran his hand over the curve of her hip.

In response, she cupped his jaw with her hand. He could feel her breath on his cheek.

And then he kissed her on the lips. Just once.

Tasha wasn't as gentle. She yanked him on top of her, and when he pressed his lips to hers again, she thrust her tongue into his mouth.

Greg's body came alive in a way it hadn't for years. He was aware of every place they were touching. Her legs between his. Her breasts against his chest. Of course, there were a couple layers of sweater between them, but still.

She arched against him, pressing against him *there*.

He growled as his cock hardened, then shifted his lips away from hers and kissed his way down to where her jaw met her neck—she'd always been particularly sensitive in that spot.

And she still was.

"Greg," she whispered, much more quietly than Ethel next door.

He loved hearing her say his name when she was underneath him.

He shifted his mouth back to Tasha's and tasted a hint of Coffee Crisp, something he'd tasted on her lips before.

"*Ethel!*"

"*Herbieee!*"

This was followed by more banging and squeaking.

Greg could feel Tasha's smile against his lips. He smiled back before cupping her ass and bringing her more firmly against him as he continued to kiss her.

It had been many, many years, but it still felt right.

Familiar, though not quite the same.

Tasha started grinding her hips against his, and he slipped his hand under her sweater and shirt, smooth skin meeting his fingertips.

He shuddered. He wanted more. He wanted—

Suddenly, they were bathed in light. What on earth was going on?

Oh, right. The power had been restored.

Greg looked down at Tasha, her braids fanned out on the pillow, her sweater pushed up, one hand gripping his shoulder.

He was making out with his ex-girlfriend.

And he'd known what he was doing, but it felt like he hadn't *really* known until now.

Tasha looked even more stunned. When he rolled off her, she shifted away from him. He missed her body heat, and not just because it was cold in the room.

"*Ethel!*"

"*Herbie!*"

A couple more bangs and it seemed to be over.

Strange that a presumably-elderly couple having sex next door during a power outage had encouraged Greg to kiss his ex. The world worked in odd ways.

He couldn't bring himself to regret it, though.

Tasha, however, still looked stunned.

"Are you okay?" he asked, not letting himself reach for her.

"Me? Oh, yeah, I'm fine. Just worried about Ethel's hip. Anyway, I'm going to head to the washroom to wrap up my hair and brush my teeth, and maybe we can go to sleep soon?"

"Sure. Of course. Yeah."

Why was he sounding like a loon?

Tasha padded across the room, and Greg lay back in the bed, feeling like his world had been knocked slightly off orbit.

He wanted to kiss her again. He wanted to lose himself in her.

But he didn't think she wanted the same thing.

Chapter 7

Tasha couldn't sleep.

She blamed it on the howling wind and the unheated motel room. She had fuzzy socks and a big sweater and several blankets, and she still didn't feel warm enough. She was even contemplating putting her toque back on, over her silk scarf.

No, she shouldn't lie to herself.

The reason she couldn't sleep was because Greg was lying next to her.

They were sharing a queen-size bed. There was a healthy distance between them, but she was quite conscious of his presence.

And he'd kissed her.

All those years ago, she'd been the one who'd kissed him first. He'd asked her on a date. It was May, and, stammering, he'd suggested a picnic.

She smiled at the memory. How many sixteen-year-old boys would pack a proper lunch—not just a bag of chips and some pop—in a wicker basket and bring it to the park by the lake? He'd made a pasta salad, and there was also a baguette and two types of cheese—cheap marble and cheddar, but still—and juice and chocolate. More than once, he'd leaned forward, and she'd thought he was going to kiss her, but he didn't.

So, finally, she'd taken matters into her own hands.

She wanted to kiss him again tonight. She wanted to do more than that, in all honesty.

It didn't have to mean anything. She'd simply found herself in bed with a handsome man from her past who could kiss the daylights out of her; they could have their fun while they were trapped in the snowstorm, then head their separate ways tomorrow.

She never got involved with an ex-boyfriend, not since Lance, but they wouldn't be getting involved.

No, they'd just have a bit of fun.

Liar.

Tasha shoved that stupid voice out of her brain. It didn't know what it was talking about.

Next to her, Greg rolled over and sighed. Apparently, he couldn't sleep, either. Hopefully it was because he, too, was thinking about their kiss.

Or possibly he was planning his next birdwatching expedition. It was hard to know.

Damn, why did she find his hobbies so endearing?

And, like, kind of sexy?

Perhaps because he was so unreservedly himself. Like in high school, when he'd never tried to fit in.

"I can't sleep," she said.

"I can't sleep, either."

Greg was thorough and detail-oriented, and it wasn't surprising he'd remembered the spot just below her jaw that she liked. He could also be rather intense, like in his hatred for Christmas music—though she could have sworn his lips had quirked up when she was singing—but she'd experienced that intensity focused on her, and there was nothing else like it.

She couldn't suppress a shudder.

"Are you cold?" he asked, his quiet, concerned voice coming through the darkness. "Do you want one of the sleeping bags? I don't think this building has very good insulation, in addition to the lack of heating. Or...never mind."

"Or, what?"

"We could cuddle." He cleared his throat. "Share body heat. You know."

"Maybe after."

"After what?"

"We have sex. If you're interested."

There was a long silence.

Yes, he'd kissed her, but maybe she'd miscalculated.

"If you don't want to, that's fine," she said in a rush. "I just figured we might as well. It wouldn't mean anything, of course, but I haven't had sex in a while, and I know we can make each other feel good, and that kiss was pretty great, wasn't it?"

Oh, no. She was babbling, and she couldn't see his expression.

And then he was on top of her, and she melted into the soft mattress.

"I'm interested," he said.

"Oh." She released a breath. "Well, then." She paused. "Shit, I don't have any condoms."

"Don't worry. I do."

Of course he did. He was prepared for everything. It only stood to reason that a guy who had two sleeping bags, a kettle, and a space heater in his trunk would also have condoms.

The mattress shifted, and she missed his weight and heat on top of her, but it wasn't long before he returned.

"I have two requests," he said.

"Yes?"

"I'd like to turn the light on so I can see you."

She wasn't usually self-conscious about her body, but Greg had seen her naked when she was young and thin and had a flat stomach.

"Tasha?" he said softly. "Is that okay?"

"I don't look like I did when I was nineteen. I've gained at least twenty-five pounds."

"So have I."

"But yours is mostly muscle." She bet he had a regimented fitness routine. That seemed like Greg. She couldn't wait to touch him all over.

"You've been checking me out, have you?"

"Yeah, when you were whining about Christmas music."

"I wasn't whining."

"Fine. Making your displeasure known in a non-whiny way."

"That's better."

"You can turn on the light," she said, "and you can touch me anywhere you want, but don't completely remove my sweater, because I'm cold."

"Anything else?" He wasn't much of a talker in the bedroom, but he'd always wanted to know how she felt and what she wanted.

"No, but you said you had a second request?"

"Yes. You can say my name, but please be quieter than Ethel and Herbie."

"That sounds soooo difficult, because I'm sure you'll make me feel soooo good."

"Tasha," he said sternly.

Ooh, she'd missed his stern voice.

"Okay, I'll behave," she said.

He flicked on the lamp by the side of the bed. "No, you won't." His dark eyes were intent on her face, and her breath came faster. "But I like it that way."

"Take off your clothes," she commanded. "All of them."

"As you wish."

"Unless you're going to be too cold."

"I'll be fine."

He pulled his shirt over his head, and she swallowed hard. He really did look good.

He smirked as she lay there admiring him, and then he stripped off his pajama pants and boxers in one smooth move. She couldn't help staring at his cock, long and heavy between his legs.

He lay on top of her again, and her sweater rode up as her arms went around him, exposing a slice of her skin to his.

"How are you so hot?" she murmured.

"May I ask which meaning of the word you're using?"

Well, both, but... "There's no heat in the room, and yet you're warm."

He tugged off her pants. His warmer legs tangled with hers, and she gasped as he rocked his hips. "I'm going to heat you up."

His hands slipped under her sweater and cupped her breasts. He rubbed the tip of one nipple between his fingers. As his mouth descended to hers, she couldn't help but imagine him doing this with other women. Being naked in bed, using his adorably stern voice on them.

No, it seemed wrong. He was hers. She'd found him first.

You're dating Greg? Her friends hadn't understood the appeal. Sure, he was decent-looking, but wasn't he a little weird?

She'd felt like she was in on some great secret.

She pushed aside her thoughts of the past, as well as her jealousy. It had been many years, and she doubted Greg had had a ton of sexual partners, but of course he'd had some—he'd had three relationships, after all.

Besides, she wouldn't have wanted him to be celibate...and perhaps he'd picked up some useful skills in that time.

She giggled as his head disappeared under her sweater. He brought the tip of one nipple into his mouth and swirled his tongue around it. Then he did something with his mouth that defied description, but it felt amazing.

His head reappeared, and he shifted up her body.

"How are you doing?" he asked.

"I'm good. Very good."

When they were younger, they'd been eager but also hesitant; it was different now. She brought her hands down to his firm ass and gave it a squeeze, not at all ashamed that this was what she wanted to do.

His palms slid over her nipples then her belly, smoothing a path down her legs, then back to her ass, and all the while he kissed her mouth in a heated yet deliberate way.

He still had a little too much control for her liking. She'd always delighted in making him lose himself, when he was normally such a sensible, measured person.

She wiggled her ass and spread her legs so his cock rubbed against the juncture of her thighs. He grunted.

She hadn't heard this particular grunt in a while, because he only made it when they were in bed together. Or in a parked car, or in a snow fort. It was the one he made when he was turned on.

She was an expert in his noises.

He continued to run his warm hands all over her cooler skin—she'd forgotten how large his hands were—and every part of her body tingled in the wake of his touch.

"How long has it been for you?" she asked suddenly.

"Oh, about four years. Since my last relationship ended."

"*Four years?*"

"Yes." His eyes danced with amusement. "Surprised?"

"Let's hope you're not rusty."

"I don't think you have to worry about that," he murmured.

"It's been four months for me."

"Mm."

"What does that mean?"

"Nothing. Just an acknowledgment of your words." He paused. "No judgment. I wanted you to have lots of, uh, experiences."

Before she could reply, he cupped her mound over her underwear. Not a particularly pretty pair, as she certainly hadn't expected this to happen.

He held her gaze, and when she nodded, he slipped them off and tossed them somewhere among all the blankets on the bed. Then he rubbed two long fingers over her entrance, groaning as he pushed them inside her. "You feel so good, Tasha."

She was practically trembling, and he wasn't even moving his fingers. Why wasn't he moving his fingers?

She circled her hips, desperate for more, and he laughed softly in her ear.

"Yes," he said, "be greedy."

And with that, his head disappeared under the covers. He licked over her slit, nice and slow.

She nearly jumped off the bed. Dear God, his mouth was incredible.

He continued to lick her as he leisurely thrust his fingers in and out, and she could hear her moisture as he moved. He nuzzled her inner thigh, his stubble rubbing over her sensitive skin.

Ohhh.

"Any complaints about my rustiness?" he asked, his words muffled by the blankets.

"No. None at all."

And then he was eating her out as though he was a starving man who hadn't eaten a meal in, well, four years. She gripped the comforter and bucked against his face, close but not quite there. And he would know that, because over the time they'd been together, he'd learned how to read her well, learned how to give her the best oral sex.

Except...what was that move? He definitely hadn't done that before.

It was sort of like... Oh, fuck. She didn't know. It just felt really good.

He lifted his mouth from her, ever so briefly, and parted her folds with his thumbs before diving back down for more.

Her grip on the comforter tightened, and she emitted a tiny squeak.

"Greg..."

He redoubled his efforts, his tongue swiping over her entrance then circling faster over her clit, and when he slipped his finger inside her and curled it, she shrieked in pleasure. She clutched his head through the blankets, holding him against her as she came.

Oh, *God*.

He threw off the blankets and crawled up her body, a crooked grin on his face.

"If you haven't done that in four years," she said, "that's a crime. Your tongue is magnificent."

She could see her moisture on his lips—and all over his chin—and she was glad he'd turned on the bedside lamp.

"Do you want more of my magnificent tongue?" he asked.

"I do believe I would."

She'd barely finished speaking before he dove back between her legs, with single-minded focus on making her feel good. At first, he was gentle, knowing she was sensitive right after she came, but then he was pumping his fingers in and out of her channel as he feasted on her. Her skin felt like it was sparking with energy, and it all coalesced into one big ball that exploded within her.

This time when he slid up her body, he pressed against her, his cock rubbing her slit. She wanted—needed—to feel it inside her; she felt achingly empty without him. She squirmed, but she couldn't move much. He was heavy, and she loved being pinned underneath him.

Now he was feasting on her neck. It felt amazing but...

"Fuck me," she said.

"Gladly."

She was gratified to see his hands shaking as he rolled on the condom. He ran the head of his cock over her entrance a few times before he adjusted himself and began to push inside. She wrapped her legs around his waist and urged him on, bucking her hips up to meet him.

He put his hand on her hip and stilled her.

"Tasha." He hissed out a breath. "Tasha, Tasha. I..."

Unable to say anything coherent, he dipped his head and kissed her as he slid the rest of the way inside. He stayed there for a moment, showering her with open-mouthed kisses, before rocking his hips against hers. It was tender at first, but achingly intense, and despite the mind-blowing oral sex, she'd been unprepared for how good this would feel. How right.

Like it was meant to be.

Taking advantage of the large bed, she tilted her hips to the left, and he rolled himself under her, his hips slamming up to meet hers. After pushing up her sweater, she cupped her breasts in her hands and circled her thumbs over her nipples.

"Yes." His gaze was riveted on her chest. "You're so..." He slammed his hips up again. "Sexy."

That was exactly how she felt.

They moved in tandem before she lowered her chest to his and picked up the pace. He thrust into her and touched his tongue to his finger. When he pressed it against her clit, she came almost immediately. Underneath her, he growled, clutching her against his body as he finished.

Well. *Well.*

It had been a long time since Greg Wong had had sex, so it wasn't surprising that it had been explosive, and he'd nearly lost his mind as soon as he slid inside the woman.

But that woman was Tasha Edwards, and he knew it wouldn't have been quite like this with anyone else.

He returned to the bedroom after disposing of the condom and put his clothes back on. Normally, he wouldn't have bothered, but sex didn't change the fact that there was no heat, except for the little provided by his tiny space heater.

He wrapped Tasha in his arms, and she snuggled back against him.

This felt like a luxury. To simply have her in his arms again.

"I missed you," he said suddenly. It was as though having sex with her had cracked something open inside him, something he'd forced closed long ago.

She hesitated. "I missed you, too."

The words hung between them for a long time.

"Look at us," she said after a while. "Snuggling together in a queen-size bed, without having to worry about any parents interrupting us. Without the sound of people funneling beer in the next room. We really are adults."

He smiled against her neck. God, he really had missed her. She'd said the sex didn't mean anything, but it didn't feel that way to him.

She started singing "Jingle Bell Rock," and he wasn't even bothered by the Christmas music. He felt dopey and relaxed, and he was content to lie here with her.

"You once did a strip show for me to 'Jingle Bell Rock,'" he said.

"I did."

All the memories of their relationship were flooding back. He hadn't allowed himself to think of them in years, but they were all there, waiting for him to want to remember.

"Do you have any regrets about us?" he asked when she finished the song. "Like, do you regret having sex when we did? Or staying together until second year? Or—"

"I don't have regrets. It's not a useful way to live life."

He supposed that fit with her optimistic, always-look-to-the-future attitude, but he made a frustrated sound. "People say that, but I think it's impossible not to have regrets."

"I don't have any regrets about you, I promise."

She turned in his arms and faced him.

He did have regrets about the two of them. He regretted that they'd broken up when they did, that they hadn't tried harder to make it work.

And yet, he'd felt like he had to let her go so she was free to experience all the world had to offer. So she could be with guys she hadn't known since kindergarten, guys who wouldn't prefer to stay in their rooms on a Saturday night and watch a documentary, but who would go out to socialize and maybe do stupid things like keg stands.

Tasha stroked her hand down his thighs.

"I'm not nineteen anymore," he said hoarsely. "It'll take more than five minutes before I'm ready for another round."

She laughed quietly, her breath against his neck.

This was definitely not how he'd imagined the day going when he'd woken up this morning. No way had he thought he'd be snowbound in a motel with Tasha, snuggling after a fantastic round of sex. But even though this hadn't been part of his plans, he was happy it had happened. Very happy.

Sure, sometimes she drove him up the wall, but it was easy to be with her, and he didn't often feel at ease with people.

Tasha cuddled closer against him. "I'm definitely all warmed up now."

"So am I."

"You were hot to begin with."

"Why thank you."

After turning off the lamp, he closed his eyes and drifted off to sleep.

Chapter 8

Tasha cracked open an eye.

The room was no longer completely dark. Light filtered in through the thin curtains and highlighted the fact that yes, this was a crappy motel room.

Her nose felt like an icicle. Still no heat.

Yet she'd awoken with a smile on her face because she'd had pretty great sex last night.

Greg.

OMG. She'd slept with Greg, and it had been fantastic.

What had she been thinking?

She threw back the covers and started to get up, but then Greg opened his eyes and mumbled, "Stay," so she did. It was warm and cozy next to him under the blankets.

Still, she was freaking out.

She'd suggested no-strings-attached, meaningless sex. She had casual sex on occasion to satisfy her needs. Nothing to feel guilty about.

The problem? It hadn't simply been sex.

No, it had been pretty freaking amazing sex.

She'd enjoyed sex with her last two boyfriends, though she'd found herself thinking, *It wasn't as good as it was with Greg.* Then she'd figured she was probably just looking at her first relationship with rose-tinted glasses. It had been more than a decade. The sex hadn't actually been that spectacular, right? After all, they were each other's firsts.

But she'd had sex with Greg last night, and it *was* that spectacular. The best she'd ever had. Maybe even better than it had been fifteen years ago. Someone should give that man's tongue a prize.

The *real* problem wasn't that the sex had been amazing, but that it had felt particularly intimate, and she'd loved it when he held her afterward. Like there was nowhere else she'd rather be than a crappy, cold motel room, as long as he was the one holding her. When he'd admitted he'd missed her, she'd said it back, and it had sent a curl of warmth to her heart. And when she thought about how he'd brought her hot chocolate and a Coffee Crisp, she grinned.

Yep, she had feelings for him.

Maybe they'd never gone away. Or maybe they had and just came back.

It didn't matter. When she looked at his glasses resting on the night-table and his argyle sweater thrown over a chair, she felt a surge of affection.

Oh, no. Did she want to get back together with her ex?

No, she couldn't.

She always looked ahead to new opportunities and experiences. Living in the past just held you back, and there was always a reason an ex was an ex. No need to revisit it.

She'd had sex without feelings before. Why couldn't it have been like that with Greg?

He wrapped his arms around her and nuzzled her neck, and ooh, that felt good. How come everything he did felt so wonderful?

She reminded herself of Crispin, who liked to laugh and respected her boundaries.

Dammit, the bar was so low. That was the problem.

Expecting men not to send you unsolicited dick pics is very reasonable, Greg had said, and she chuckled at the memory.

Really, she didn't understand why he didn't do well with online dating. Compared to all the jerks out there, he was practically a saint.

She sat up.

"What's the rush?" he murmured. "I'll get you home by noon, don't worry. Might as well wait under the covers for now and give them a chance to clear the roads."

His warm mouth pressed against her collarbone, then her neck.

"Look at you." She forced a laugh. "Yesterday, you were so eager to get on the road, pissed that I was twenty-seven minutes late, and now you want to lie in bed and *snuggle*." She said it with fake disdain.

"Yes, I'm always DTS," he said. "Down to snuggle."

She laughed for real.

Greg had always been a cuddly person, though it seemed counter to his personality. Surely this wasn't just with her, but with other women, too.

She pushed that thought aside. She didn't want to think about his girlfriends.

Though maybe that would help her move on.

"Tasha," he said, serious now. "Do you regret last night?"

"No regrets, like I said." She gave him a peck on the lips and hopped out of bed. "I need a shower. Hopefully there's warm water."

He looked at her for a moment, his face carefully blank. "Okay. I think there's a Tim Hortons nearby. I'll get us some breakfast and see what the roads are like. You still take your coffee the same way?"

She nodded and forced back the tears.

He remembered how she took her coffee. Really, it was nothing.

But he also remembered how she liked to be touched, and so many other things. It was just the way he was. He was careful and kind and remembered little things.

Dear God, how had this happened?

Breakfast sandwiches, coffee, and Timbits.

Simple. He could do this.

Greg stepped out of the motel room and into the bright sunshine reflecting off the snowbanks. He'd have to dig out his car first. That might take a while. Fortunately he had two shovels in the trunk—all part of his winter preparedness kit.

A door creaked, and an older white man walked out of the next room. He looked a little older than Greg's parents, though it was hard to tell as he was wearing a big parka.

Oh, God. This was *Herbie.*

Greg knew what sounds this man made in the bedroom. At least, he knew the tone of voice Herbie used when he said, "Ethel."

This was wrong, so wrong.

And Herbie may well have heard the bed springs creaking in Greg and Tasha's room last night, maybe even some of Tasha's noises. She hadn't been too loud, but the walls were thin.

"Hello, *Greg,*" Herbie said with a wink. "Have a good night?"

Well, at least Tasha hadn't called him "Greggie," but it was like finding yourself naked in a classroom. Not, of course, that this had ever happened to Greg, but he'd had dreams—nightmares, really—of that situation.

Someone else may have been able to breezily reply, *Pretty good, Herbie. And you?*

But Greg was not that smooth.

Herbie laughed. "Big storm last night, eh?"

"Yes."

"Me and the wife, we were heading to Hamilton to see our daughter, but we had to get off the 402 during the storm."

Herbie prattled on for a few minutes, and Greg was unable to drag himself out of the conversation. Then a woman stepped outside and linked her arm with Herbie's, and Greg was hit with an unexpected surge of longing.

He wanted to be like them one day. A couple in their seventies, heading out to spend Christmas with their adult children. An older couple who still had very enthusiastic sex. He couldn't look Herbie and Ethel in the eye, but he couldn't help wanting what they had.

With Tasha.

It was impossible to imagine being with anyone but Tasha now.

He mumbled a hasty goodbye, headed to his car, and pulled out a shovel. He shoveled like mad, hoping the physical exertion would drown out his thoughts.

But it didn't.

The crack that had opened within him last night had widened.

He wanted to be with Tasha. Not just for one night in a heat-free motel room. Not just for a few months or years.

He wanted to be with her for always.

Perhaps he'd never stopped loving her; perhaps he'd merely managed to repress those feelings so he could move on with his life, and whenever they'd manage to pop up again, he'd forced them back down, telling himself he was just nostalgic for his teenage years. Once or twice, he'd picked up the phone to call her, then convinced himself he was being silly. Besides, she hadn't bothered to contact him; surely she'd moved on to better things.

But it was now startlingly clear why his other three relationships hadn't worked out. Why he hadn't bothered dating for the past few years.

He'd never been able to imagine far into the future with another woman like he could with Tasha; for him, no one could compare to her. After last night, he knew it wasn't foolish nostalgia. They were good together. They really were. He belonged with her; he knew this with a certainty he'd never had before.

At nineteen, he'd had trouble believing she'd pick him if she could see what else was out there, but now she was thirty-four and still unattached. If she chose him now, after fifteen more years of life experience... Well, that would be different.

There was one big problem, however.

He didn't think she wanted him.

Sure, she'd cuddled up against Greg last night and said she missed him, but this morning, she'd been eager to leave the comfort of the bed and had shown no interest in having sex again.

She'd said she didn't regret it—and maybe she didn't. She'd clearly enjoyed herself. But she didn't seem thrilled about the current situation, and there was no reason to think she'd be interested in anything more. After all, she'd stated, just yesterday, that she didn't believe in second chances for relationships.

Besides, even though she didn't have a husband or boyfriend, she had that Crispin guy, who probably even liked Christmas music.

That asshole.

Half an hour later, Greg finally had his car cleared off, and, with some difficulty, he managed to get it out of the parking lot and down the road to the nearest Tim Hortons. He bought two breakfast sandwiches, a double-double (for Tasha), a black coffee (for him), and a box of ten Timbits.

He was about to head back outside when his phone buzzed.

"Hey, Greg!" Nick said when Greg picked up.

He set down his order on a table and rubbed his forehead. This was just what he needed.

"Why are you calling?" Greg asked.

"Gee, thanks for the warm hello."

"You know I prefer texting."

"I figured this would be more efficient."

"Does everyone in the household want to talk to me again?"

"Yeah, something like that."

Greg grunted in frustration. "I'll be home in a couple hours. You can all bother me then."

"Don't worry. I'm sure that'll happen, too."

Nick got off the phone, and then a different voice said, "So, Greg, did anything happen last night?"

"Mom. Please. I'm starting to worry that you can control the weather, and that's how I ended up trapped in a motel room near Strathroy with my ex-girlfriend, next to two septuagenarians having wild sex."

He didn't know why he added that last part. His brain really wasn't working today.

Mom laughed. "Your grandfather wants to talk to you."

A moment later, Ah Yeh said, "I discovered that you can buy model trees on Amazon. Just the right size for your train set. Should I get cedars or palm trees, or the set of mixed trees? There are dozens of options, actually."

"I have all the model trees I need, thank you," Greg said.

Eventually, he managed to end the call, then took his food and coffee out to the car. He put on CBC Radio, just because there was no one to tell him not to, even though it was only a short drive.

When he returned to the motel, Tasha was dressed in a blue sweater that was slightly more form-fitting than the one she'd worn yesterday. She immediately grabbed the Timbit box and popped one of the donut holes in her mouth.

"Mmmm," she said.

He looked on, horrified.

"What?" she asked.

"I got you a breakfast sandwich, but you're eating dessert first."

"I don't think appetizers, main courses, and desserts apply at breakfast. Breakfast is a free-for-all." She grinned as she dumped two creams and sugars into her coffee.

He had a sip of his own coffee and smiled. He would never eat a donut before his breakfast sandwich—that just wasn't the way he did things—but he appreciated that she didn't follow such rigid rules.

"I'm surprised you bought donuts," she said. "I figured that was too indulgent for you, especially at Christmas. I know there's a ton of dessert at your family's house this time of year."

He shrugged. "You like them. So I got some."

The smile slid off her face and she was back to looking like she had earlier this morning, when she refused to stay burrowed under the covers with him.

"What's wrong?" He yearned to reach out and caress her cheek, but he kept his hands to himself.

"Nothing's wrong," she said brightly, then turned to look out the window.

He studied her profile. She really was the prettiest woman he'd ever known.

He loved the faint wrinkles and stretch marks, the fact that her body wasn't exactly the same as it had been before. She could pass for being younger than thirty-four, but she was a little different from her teenage self, and he liked being able to see that time had passed. She was still *Tasha*, but now she had the career she'd worked so hard for. He'd have to ask her more about her job on the ride back.

She'd also admitted she wanted a relationship, and he wanted to give that to her.

Except she didn't seem keen on being with him for more than a night.

"Did you talk to Crispin this morning?" he asked, unable to keep the edge out of his voice.

"No." She held up a Timbit and changed the topic. "I dare you to eat one of these before your breakfast sandwich."

He grimaced.

"Oh, come on. It's just a donut. Live a little."

It seemed she was bent on torturing him again: she had his least favorite Timbit in her hand.

"Powdered...sugar," he stammered.

Greg hated powdered sugar. It probably had something to do with a little incident that happened when he was three years old. His grandfather—his mother's father, who'd been dead for a dozen years now—had taken him to a bakery in a nearby town, and somehow he'd ended up with a large donut covered in powdered sugar. Not just a little donut hole—no, a full donut. Greg had gleefully bitten into the donut and waved it around in the air...and started crying when the powdered sugar got all over his favorite sweater. Most kids probably wouldn't have been bothered, but Greg had always been concerned with neatness and order, even from a young age, and he'd thrown a temper tantrum in the bakery.

Anyway, he still hated powdered sugar because it was messy. This particular donut, he knew, had jelly inside. That was tasty, but the powdered sugar he could do without.

At the same time, he kind of wanted to eat it now, before his sandwich. Show Tasha that he wasn't a total stick-in-the-mud.

"Alright," she said. "No powdered sugar. Sour cream glazed instead." She held up another Timbit, once that was mercifully less messy. "I dare you to eat one sour cream glazed Timbit before your breakfast sandwich."

Everything in him tensed at the thought of eating dessert first. It went against the rules, and Greg loved the rules.

Though he missed having a little chaos in his life.

His childhood had been too full of chaos. He was the oldest of four, and his parents hadn't exactly run a structured, ordered household. There was always one catastrophe or another, someone shrieking in his ear.

But his life in Toronto had gotten a little boring, to be honest.

"Sour cream glazed is the best one," Tasha said, shaking the Timbit.

"I thought birthday cake was your favorite."

She shrugged. "People change."

Well, yes, and Tasha changing her Timbit preference didn't fundamentally change who she was, whereas him eating a jelly donut covered in powdered sugar, while wearing a pristine argyle sweater, seemed a little more of a stretch.

"Pass me the jelly one," he said.

She raised her eyebrows and handed it over.

Greg held it close to his face. Geez, this was one messy fucker of a donut. Nothing should be dipped in powdered sugar—or cocoa powder, for that matter—and it seemed like this particular donut had an extra-generous amount of powdered sugar.

He was going to eat this. He had to. Somehow, it seemed like eating this little donut symbolized something important.

All in one bite—that was probably the best way to minimize the mess.

He looked down at his sweater, which he didn't want to get dirty before nine in the morning. It was, in fact, his favorite sweater. He wasn't sure whether it was weird for a thirty-four-year-old man to have a favorite sweater, but he did.

And then he had an idea.

Chapter 9

Tasha didn't understand what was going on.

Greg was staring at the donut as though it contained the solution to climate change. Then one corner of his mouth quirked up, and his expression changed from thoughtful to mischievous.

She was a sucker for that look.

He put the Timbit down.

Huh? If he wasn't going to accept her challenge to eat a donut before his breakfast sandwich, then why the playful look?

He slid his thumb and finger into his mouth and sucked off the powdered sugar, holding her gaze the whole time, before wiping his hands on his corduroys.

Next, he pulled off his sweater and collared shirt and threw them on the bed.

What on earth was happening? He was going to get hypothermia in this freezing room.

Well, that was a bit of an exaggeration, but...

"You'll be cold," she said.

"For thirty seconds. I'll survive."

She dropped her gaze from his eyes to his chest. He looked quite nice without a shirt, a light dusting of hair covering his muscled chest. "Are you trying to seduce me again?"

"Again? You're the one who propositioned me last night."

"You kissed me first," she said accusingly.

"After you touched my face."

"If you're not trying to seduce me, why are you half-naked?"

"So I can eat this donut without getting powdered sugar all over my sweater." He spoke as though this was the most sensible thing in the world.

"I offered you a sour cream glazed donut. Why didn't you eat that one?"

"I decided to live dangerously."

And with those un-Greg-like words, he popped the whole Timbit into his mouth.

There was zero mess. He hadn't needed to remove his shirt, not that she didn't appreciate the view.

He wiped his fingers on his chest, right above his nipple. "You want a taste?"

"I thought you weren't trying to seduce me."

"Maybe I changed my mind."

"Nah, doesn't sound like you. I bet this was part of your plan all along."

She couldn't help herself. She leaned forward and swirled her tongue over his nipple. He made a strangled noise in his throat—he'd always had sensitive nipples.

When he kissed her mouth, tasting of sugar and jelly, she dragged him back to bed.

"Holy smokes, it really did snow a lot," Tasha said as they stepped outside. It was like a winter wonderland out here. "Must have taken a while for you to clean off your car. You should have asked me to help."

Greg shrugged. "You were showering. It's no big deal, though it would have been easier had it been drier snow." He picked up a clump of snow in his bare hands, formed a snowball, and tossed it on the ground. "I'll pay for the room, and then—"

"No. We took your car. You bought the gas, plus you provided breakfast and dinner. I'll pay for the room. It's half-price, anyway."

"Very well."

Ten minutes later, they were on their way to Mosquito Bay. The roads weren't great, but at least it wasn't snowing anymore and there were no visibility problems. The sky was a brilliant blue, and Tasha ought to be happy.

She was going home for Christmas. She'd been looking forward to this for weeks. But as she looked out over the snow-covered fields, there was an emptiness inside her.

Their road trip was only supposed to be three hours. Certainly no more than four or five. Instead, they'd had to spend the night in a motel during a snowstorm.

Yet she was sad it was coming to an end. Her time with Greg was almost over.

No more arguing about Christmas music. No more pillow talk when the power was out. No one to bring her a Coffee Crisp and kiss behind her ear and go down on her under the covers.

She shook her head. This was ridiculous.

They were listening to CBC now, and Greg's gaze was firmly on the road—as it should be. She looked at him in profile, his glasses perched on his nose.

God, why did she find him so attractive? There were a few strands of gray at his temples, and those made her smile. Why?

He was stubborn and serious...except when he wasn't, and did silly things like take off his shirt to eat a donut. He was the same Greg he'd been in high school and university...except not quite. He'd grown up. They'd both grown up. And apparently grown-up Tasha was still wildly attracted to Greg Wong.

Being with him didn't *feel* like she was living in the past, but she couldn't start something up with him again.

Or could she? Maybe?

She pulled out her phone and texted Monique. *I slept with him. Twice.*

Tasha! I told you…

I know, I know.

Oh, honey. What were you thinking? Now I don't want to wish bad sex on you, but I kind of hope it was like kissing a frog. Or toad. Or salamander.

Glad you know your amphibians.

I do my best.

The sex was good, Tasha said. *It was more than sex, actually. I might want him back.*

There. She'd admitted it. Now Monique would talk some sense back into her brain.

No!! her friend said. *After Lance, you swore you'd never get back together with an ex, remember? You told me not to get back together with Joey, and I wish I'd listened to you. We broke up for exactly the same reasons the second time. You don't want to make the same mistake twice, like me.*

Tasha didn't consider her long-ago relationship with Greg a mistake; as she'd told him, she had no regrets. But

Monique was right. You learned from what happened and moved on. Reuniting with an ex never ended well.

We're going out on New Year's Eve, Monique said, *and we're going to meet cute guys. No assholes or exes. Unless you're still seeing Crispin?*

Oh, Crispin. Tasha couldn't go out with him again. Being with him was nothing like Greg. Greg was wonderful, and the woman who ended up with him would be lucky indeed, but he wasn't for Tasha. She needed to listen to her friend and let this go.

However, as they got closer and closer to Mosquito Bay, she couldn't bear the thought of being separated from him. It was only ten thirty. They could stay together a little longer, couldn't they?

But what could they do?

Ah. She had it. The ground was covered in snow, and it was good packing snow.

She turned to Greg. "Want to build a snow fort?"

Greg hated when people changed their plans on him.

The plan had been to drive back to Mosquito Bay and drop Tasha off at her parents' house, then go home to his obnoxiously loud family.

He wanted to see his family. He did.

He just wasn't in the mood for them right now.

No, he'd do anything to spend more time with Tasha. He was glad she'd suggested a snow fort. It sounded perfect, even if they were too old for this. Building a decent snow fort would take a while.

"Sure," he said. "Let's do it."

When they entered Mosquito Bay, instead of continuing along Main Street, he drove to the park overlooking the water and parked nearby on the street. Then he texted Nick. *Won't be home for a couple more hours. Don't worry. We're safe.*

Then he turned off his phone, expecting an avalanche of texts in response.

"Alright," he said. "Are we going to build a snow fort shaped like an igloo? Or just something with high walls, like the one I made for you in university?"

He couldn't believe he was doing this. Usually if Greg spent so much time with one person, he started to go a little nuts, but he didn't want to be separated from Tasha again.

She'd freaked out this morning, but maybe this snow fort business was a sign that she was changing her mind about him.

He couldn't help but hope.

She smiled at him, and it hit him right in the chest. Goddammit, how had he gone so long without her?

"We won't make it very big," she said, "but tall enough so no one can see inside. It'll be like Rapunzel's tower."

"Why don't you want anyone to see inside?" He waggled his eyebrows.

"Oh, no reason." She was already climbing out of the car, but she winked at him over her shoulder.

For a long time, they worked in silence, starting with the base of their snow tower and building upward. He enjoyed simply being in her presence, doing something with her. It was a bright winter day. Cold, but not frigid, and it didn't bother him at all, as long as he got to be with her, and perhaps make out with her inside the snow fort afterward.

"Greg," Tasha said suddenly, "are you humming 'Winter Wonderland'?"

He realized in horror that he was, indeed, humming a Christmas song.

But he just shrugged and kept on humming.

At long last, their snow fort/tower was ready. Greg grabbed one of the sleeping bags from his car. He threw the sleeping bag into the snow fort first, then crawled in. Tasha followed him and rolled their giant snowball door in front of the entrance.

They were all alone, surrounded by snow.

"It's smaller than the snow fort you made in university," she said. "How long did it take you to build that one, all by yourself?"

"A long time."

Tasha was sitting next to him, both of them with their knees bent, their sides touching—there wasn't much space in here. It was quite cozy.

He wouldn't have it any other way.

He unzipped the sleeping bag and put it over them like a blanket before wrapping his arms around her. Most of her skin was covered by winter clothes, but he kissed her where he could. Her ear, her nose, her temple. He pushed her scarf down and kissed the top of her neck. And with every kiss, he thought, *I love this part of you...and this part...and this part. I love that you drive me crazy. I love that you've accomplished what you set out to do in life. I love that you didn't compromise your dream for me.*

She kissed him, too. His cheek, his nose. Fortunately, he'd already safely stowed his glasses away.

They were in their own little world, blue sky and sunshine above them, and he didn't ever want to leave, even if it was cold. Because as long as they were here, it was just the two of them; the rest of the world didn't matter. As long as they were here, she would be in his arms.

He sucked on her bottom lip, and then they were kissing each other as though their lives depended on it, her mouth so sweet against his; faintly, he could taste the donuts they'd indulged in earlier, and he smiled.

He wanted all kinds of kisses with her. Inside-a-snow-fort kisses. Goodnight kisses. Hello kisses. Goodbye-I'm-leaving-for-work-and-I'll-see-you-this-evening kisses. Please-stop-listening-to-CBC-programming-so-we-can-fuck kisses.

But what if this was all he'd have?

She fumbled with the zipper on his pants, then slipped her hand inside and wrapped her hand around the length of him. Her face was so close to his, watching him. Could she tell how he felt?

She pumped him harder, and he bucked his hips.

He needed to touch her, too.

When he slid his fingers inside her, she was warm and wet for him. Even after all this time, even when they were outside in the snow, she wanted him, and he was in awe of it. He stroked her slowly, the catches in her breath magnified in the little snow tower.

"How are we going to do this?" she asked.

"How are we going to fuck, you mean."

"Yeah." She giggled. "I love when you say that word."

"Do you? I can use it more often." He paused. "I think *fucking* would work best with you on my lap."

She pushed her pants and underwear down to her knees. It wouldn't be possible to get them any further off. Plus, it was cold.

But they had each other's body heat.

He rolled on the condom he'd stashed in his pocket, and she lifted herself up on her knees and lined up the tip of his cock with her entrance. Slowly, she sank down on him, and he tipped his head back and groaned.

Christ, she felt amazing.

He opened his eyes, and her face was right above his. Her lips parted in pleasure as she began to move.

Even if she walked away when this was over, he'd always feel inextricably linked to her.

He'd always belong to her.

He kissed her as she sank down on his cock again and again, her arms wrapped around him, her mitten-covered hands on the back of his neck. There was too much clothing for his liking, but still, they were together.

He took off his glove, licked his finger, and circled it over her clit. Their breaths came faster and faster. When she shattered, he held her tight and he pumped into her a few more times, finding his own release inside her.

They hadn't talked on the walk back to his car, and they hadn't talked during the short drive to her family's house.

Now, they were sitting in the driveway, their time together coming to a close.

"Tasha," he said, "I had a good time with you these past twenty-three hours and six minutes. Would you..." He swallowed. He couldn't manage to say everything he felt, everything he wanted, so he went with, "Would you want to see me again while we're both in town for the holidays? Go out for coffee and Timbits at Tim Hortons, perhaps?"

She met his gaze before looking down.

"Maybe," she said at last.

It wasn't a no, but not quite what he'd hoped for. Even as he felt a heaviness in his chest, he couldn't help wanting to make her smile. "You know who I met when I left the motel room to go to Tim Hortons? Herbie."

To his delight, she did smile.

"He called me by my name," Greg continued, "without me introducing myself."

She kissed him one more time, and then she left.

Chapter 10

"Tasha!" Her mother threw her arms around her the minute she stepped in the door. "You're finally here."

"It's so good to see you, Mom."

Tasha tried to sound upbeat. After all, she really was happy to see her mother. It had been more than two months, though they talked on the phone several times a week.

When Tasha was younger, people had often commented on her resemblance to her father, but as she got older, she looked more and more like her mother—the shape of her features, the warn undertones in her skin. Her wide smile.

"You look like you're freezing," Mom said. "Did that boy's car not have any heat?"

"Oh, there was heat," Tasha said.

Mom raised her eyebrows.

Tasha shrugged. "I'm going to make hot chocolate. You want some?"

They sat by the fire, drank their hot chocolate, and caught up on what had happened—well, some of it. But

Tasha couldn't help feeling cold on the inside, and there was nothing she could do about it, no matter how many hot beverages she drank.

Maybe having sex in a snow fort wasn't such a great idea after all.

"Where's Dad?" she asked.

"He's at Lawrence's, trying to fix their car."

Tasha had two older brothers, her father's sons from his first marriage. Her parents had met when they were in their mid-thirties, both of them divorced. Her mother's first marriage had been to her high school sweetheart, who'd discouraged her from trying to go to med school like she'd wanted. Instead, she'd become a nurse, which he'd considered a more suitable career for his wife.

That was why her mother never wanted Tasha to compromise her dreams for a man. Why she'd been worried about Tasha having a serious relationship in high school, although she hadn't forbidden her from dating.

"We had a good time together, Greg and I," Tasha ventured at last.

"Did you, now. What, exactly, did you do?"

Tasha looked down at her nearly-empty mug and tried to hide her smile. "He wants to see me again while we're both in Mosquito Bay for the holidays."

"And you said?"

"Maybe."

"Hmm."

It was irritating when her mom did that.

"What?" Tasha asked.

"If you had a good time together," Mom said slowly, "then why don't you know if you want to see him again?"

"Because he's my ex! It ended once before."

Mom didn't say anything, just sipped her hot chocolate.

"I'm thirty-four," Tasha said. "I don't want to waste time on having a little fun. I'd like to settle down."

She thought she'd have someone by now. Instead, people would kindly pat her on the back and tell her that she'd find a man soon enough. They might also tell her to lower her expectations. Or try harder.

And she wanted to tear her hair out in frustration. Had these people seen what the dating market was like? Even finding a half-decent guy seemed like a miracle, never mind someone who gave her a spark.

Which she had with Greg. Oh, she definitely did.

"You think I should give him another chance?" she asked.

"It doesn't matter what I want," Mom said. "It's what you want."

Tasha groaned, and her mom laughed.

"We fight all the time," Tasha said.

"But do you really?"

"Well..." She supposed her mom had a point. They hadn't fought about the big things, the important things. They bantered about stupid shit like Christmas carols. And all couples fought sometimes—even her parents. There was nothing wrong with that. "But I can't get back together with an ex. Everyone knows that doesn't turn out well, and it was a disaster for me and Lance. Why should I think this is different?"

"Why did you and Greg break up the first time?"

"Because we were going to different schools and drifting apart. I also didn't like the idea of having only been with one guy, you know? I was nineteen, and I thought I should get more experience."

"But all of that's changed now. You have jobs in the same city."

"Still, I can't help thinking that if it was meant to be, we would have figured it out the first time."

Though it was nothing like Monique and Joey. He'd screwed up, she'd broken up with him. Then later she forgave him and let him have another chance, and he'd screwed up again. It was a similar story with Tasha and Lance. She'd needed him to change, and he hadn't.

Greg had changed a little over the years, but he was still basically the same—and in his case, that was good. He'd always treated her well.

Tasha shoved her hands into her hair. "I don't know."

"I don't, either," Mom said, "but you shouldn't refuse to consider him just because second chances have failed in the past."

Perhaps her mother had a point.

A lot of things had worked out well for Tasha. She loved her career now. The work environment at her previous job hadn't been ideal, but she was happy with her current job, and she had good friends in Toronto.

Everything had worked out except her love life.

She didn't let herself have regrets. Look forward, never back. That was how she lived. Part of the reason for this was that after her break-up with Greg, she'd wallowed for several weeks, replaying all of their time together in her head, wondering if they'd done the right thing. Then she'd picked herself up and moved on with her life, and she'd started to feel more like herself again.

Still, she'd thought of Greg over the years. In fact, she'd found herself thinking, *It wasn't as good as it was with Greg* many times—and not just about sex. And every time, she'd assumed she was wrong.

But now, they'd spent almost twenty-four hours together. Now, she knew she hadn't been kidding herself.

It really was good with Greg.

She'd told herself they were too different, they weren't compatible. And yes, they were opposites in some ways, but saying they weren't compatible would be a lie. A lie that she'd told herself so she could move on.

But maybe, in this case, looking to the past was the best way forward.

As soon as Greg opened the door to his childhood home, everyone descended on him.

"What took you so long?" Nick asked. "Were you off making out somewhere?"

"So, how'd it go, lover boy?" That was Zach. "Did you have a good time getting trapped in that snowstorm?"

"I made the snowstorm happen!" Ah Ma said. "I have magic powers!"

Dad rolled his eyes. "Ma, surely if you had magic powers you would use some of them to improve your cooking."

She sniffed. "They are very *specific* magic powers. For love."

"Greg," Mom said, "why didn't you bring Tasha here for a little visit?"

"She wanted to see her family."

Perhaps he spoke a little irritably. Everyone was giving him funny looks now.

"You know," Nick said, putting one arm around Lily's shoulder, "I'm an expert at relationships now. If you need any advice, just ask."

"A two-and-a-half-month relationship does not make you an expert," Zach said.

"I have been married over sixty years!" Ah Ma raised her hand in the air. "I am the true expert. Plus, I have magic powers. Please, tell your ah ma what happened." She gestured to her ear. "You can tell me, no one else. I will keep your secret!"

"You are terrible at keeping secrets," Dad said. "What about the time—"

"Enough," Greg howled, and everyone stared at him, not used to hearing him speak so loudly. "I asked if I could see her again, she said maybe, end of story. Now, please leave me alone."

"I'll heat up some food for you," Mom said.

Finally, a suggestion he actually liked.

He spent ten minutes eating his grandfather's famous noodles while his family jabbered around him. Normally, he would enjoy his food—Ah Yeh's noodles were delicious. But right now, he just wanted to take off his sweater and eat another donut covered in powdered sugar.

Jesus. He really was losing it.

Afterward, he stalked upstairs to his childhood bedroom and closed the door. There wasn't much in his old room. Just the furniture remained. All the *stuff* had been cleared out long ago.

Except for one red gift box in the bottom drawer of the dresser.

He pulled it out and sat down on his bed as he looked at the contents.

For Valentine's Day in their final year of high school, Tasha had gotten him a box of valentines. Not just one or two—no, she'd gotten him fifty valentines, all with handwritten messages. It must have taken her ages.

He couldn't bear to throw them out, but he hadn't wanted them with him in Toronto. So he kept them here.

It had been many years since he'd looked at them, but now he took them out, one at a time. There was a *Lady and the Tramp* valentine, another with a cute puffin, one with a terrible chemistry joke.

"Whatcha doing?" Nick asked, waltzing into the room without knocking.

A man couldn't get a minute's peace around here, could he?

"Nothing," Greg muttered, shoving the box under the quilt.

"Sure doesn't look like nothing."

"Things Tasha gave me in high school, that's all. None of your business."

"Fine, fine. I won't pry into your life."

That didn't sound like his family.

He waited for Nick to try to grab the box, but it didn't happen.

"I was jealous of you in high school," Nick said.

Greg snorted. "You? Jealous of me?"

"Yeah, why not? You weren't cool—"

"Gee, thanks," Greg muttered, but Nick's words were just a statement of fact. He had never been cool, not one bit.

"—but you didn't care what anyone else thought, and you had a girlfriend."

"Did you have a crush on Tasha?"

"Nah, I was just envious that you got a girl's attention."

Right. It was hard to remember that back in the day, Nick hadn't been popular. High school was so long ago now.

Greg and Tasha...also so long ago.

But he didn't want to be with her simply because he had fond memories of the past. They'd spent time together as adults now, and he'd enjoyed every minute of it, even when she'd insisted on singing "The Twelve Days of Christmas."

"You slept with her, didn't you?" Nick pulled up a chair and sat on it backward.

Greg grunted.

"I'll take that as a yes."

"Why don't you take it as a none-of-your-business?"

Just then, the door opened again, and their father stepped into the room.

"If you want to have a party," Greg muttered, "could you please do it somewhere else?"

"He's moping over Tasha," Nick said.

"That's what I figured." Dad took a seat on the bed next to Greg. "I liked you and Tasha together. You complemented each other. I thought you'd be like me and your mom."

Greg grunted again.

"You know," Dad said, "we didn't date continuously from the time we started going out in grade eleven. At one point, we took a break for several months."

Greg had to admit he was a little intrigued by this.

"We were eighteen," Dad continued. "Not quite sure what we wanted. There was another guy who was interested in her... Anyway, that didn't last. I'm just saying, when you fall in love when you're so young and you don't really know yourself yet, it can be tricky. I still think it could work out for you."

"Hmm."

"Sometimes it's useful to speak actual words," Nick said.

"I can't think clearly while I'm talking."

Nick and Dad were quiet for a minute. It was still difficult for Greg to think properly when he wasn't alone, but yes, he did want to see Tasha again. Desperately. He loved her; he loved who she'd become.

"So tell me what happened," Nick said, breaking the silence. "The weekend went well, and you casually asked if you could see her again, maybe meet up for coffee?"

"That's right," Greg said. "She said no."

"Not that there's anything wrong with what you did—"

"Glad it meets your approval."

"—but you aren't the most eloquent person," Nick finished. "Maybe you need to really show her how you feel. Not sexually, though."

"Thanks for the clarification."

"Like, show her that you don't just want to grab coffee together, but you want more. Because you do, right?"

"Yeah." So much more.

"And, like, you're both getting old. I mean, you're thirty-four—"

"I know how old I am."

"And she's probably looking to settle down, maybe have kids. It's different from when you were teenagers."

Zach walked into the room. "What are we talking about?"

"Trying to find something nice for Greg to do for Tasha."

"Excellent. Maybe you could set up a special model train for her. Like, make it go through a love forest. Or love mountain."

"Um," Greg said.

Tasha would probably think it was cute, but it would take far too much time to get all the materials and set it up. He needed a better idea.

She'd said she didn't believe in second chances for relationships, but he had to try one last time. Tell her how he truly felt. Put it all out there.

"What about a really big cookie?" Nick suggested.

"That's your genius idea? Just one big cookie?"

"Everyone loves cookies. You baked a few times for Tasha, I remember."

"You could go birdwatching together," Zach said, "and, uh, find a really great bird for her. Or put up a banner under the sign for Mosquito Bay."

"No," Nick said. "Too public. He won't go for that."

Mom and Amber entered the room.

"What are we doing?" Mom asked.

Greg pinched his forehead in frustration, then walked over to the window and looked outside. The blue sky and sunshine were gone. Instead, it was overcast, and it looked like it could possibly snow again—and more snow was just what they needed.

Though he had an odd affection for snowstorms now, having been trapped in one with Tasha Edwards.

All that snow gave him an idea.

"I know what to do," he said, turning to his family, "but I'm going to need some help."

Everyone nodded.

His family drove him batshit crazy, but he could always count on them.

"Okay, here's the plan."

It was almost midnight. Tasha's parents had gone to bed.

As a child, she'd bounced with excitement on Christmas Eve, looking forward to Santa Claus's arrival and wishing for the best presents. She'd always tried to stay up late so she could see Santa and his reindeer, but she'd never made it.

Now, she was holding the gold necklace that she'd stashed in her ballerina jewelry box many years before. There was no other jewelry in the box, just the necklace.

The one that had made Greg hate Christmas music.

For two years, she'd worn it every day. She would squeeze her fist around it when she suddenly, inexplicably, felt a wave of longing for him during a lecture or lab.

Just like the way she longed for him now.

She wrapped her hand around the pendant and made her Christmas wish.

Chapter 11

On Christmas morning, Tasha was eating pancakes with maple syrup and drinking her second cup of coffee when there was a knock at the door.

"I'll get it." Her father started to stand, but he wasn't as spry as he'd once been.

"No, I will." Tasha jumped up, hoping it was Greg.

But it wasn't.

The man looked a bit like Greg, but he was a couple inches shorter and wasn't wearing glasses. Plus, his smile was all wrong.

"Nick?" Tasha said. She hadn't seen him in years.

"Hey, Tasha."

Why was Nick on the doorstep?

"Is something the matter?" Her words came out in a rush.

"No, everything's fine. I just have something to show you. Can you come with me now? Or if you want to spend Christmas morning with your family..." He peeked inside and waved at her parents.

"I'll go."

She gulped down the rest of her coffee, hugged her mom and dad, put on her winter clothes, and headed outside with Nick. It was a nice morning, like it had been yesterday. Partly sunny with some clouds in the sky. Not much wind coming off the lake.

Nick led her down Main Street, where the lampposts were decorated with wreaths, then down another street, toward Lake Huron.

Compared to Toronto, it was a tiny speck of a town. Neither of her parents were from Mosquito Bay, but it was in between her father's old auto shop and the hospital where her mom had worked. It was also not far from where her father's ex-wife had lived, so it was easy for him to see his sons.

Tasha hadn't minded growing up here, though she hadn't looked like most of the other kids. But she preferred her life in Toronto, only coming back to visit her family.

"Where are we going?" she asked Nick, hugging her arms around herself.

"Almost there," he said.

She refused to hope too much, but she had a feeling...

They entered the park where she and Greg had made the snow fort yesterday. There were a bunch of kids sledding on the hill, a few kids making a snowman, and some people standing around, looking at—

What on earth?

Their little snow tower was now part of the most magnificent snow fort she'd ever seen. It was like a castle.

Her gloved hand came up to her face. "He did this for me? How long did it take?"

"Oh, he didn't do it all himself. He had help. We spent most of yesterday outside. My whole family, aside from my grandparents. It's Greg's design, and we had to listen to him be a control freak all day." Nick was smiling, though. They kept walking toward the snow fort, until they reached a little doorway, not tall enough to walk through. "Go inside and turn right."

She gave Nick a hug, then did as he said. She got down on her hands and knees and crawled into the snow fort. The short entryway was covered, but other than that, there was no roof. The walls to the right were at least six feet tall, though. She continued crawling, her heart beating rapidly, and when she turned the corner, she saw Greg.

He was sitting on a sleeping bag, and there was a little picnic basket next to him. In the snow fort he'd built just for her.

"Come here," he said.

When she knelt beside him, he pulled a thermos out of the basket and poured her some hot chocolate. The steam curled in the cold air.

"I have something to tell you," he said, "if you'd like to listen, that is."

She nodded.

He looked very serious, despite the fact that he was wearing a red down jacket and gray toque and sitting in a snow fort. He opened a tin of homemade chocolate chip cookies and handed one to her.

She took a bite. It was delicious.

"I..." He took off his glasses and scrubbed a hand over his face. "Okay. Here it goes." But he didn't say anything more. He seemed to be quietly freaking out.

He pulled a sheet of paper out of his pocket. Had he written a speech?

Something swelled in her chest, and she smiled at him encouragingly.

"I want to clarify what I said yesterday," he said, tucking away the paper. "I asked if I could see you again while we were both here for the holidays, but you should know that I want a lot more than that. We only had twenty-three hours and six minutes together, after fifteen years of hardly seeing each other, but it was enough. Enough to remember all the things I love about you. Enough to learn how you've changed, and how you haven't. I want to know every detail of the life you've created, Tasha, and I want to be a part of it. I want another chance at a relationship. I'm not just a kid anymore, and..." His voice turned hoarse. "I'm serious about you. I do want to get married and have children together and all that stuff we used to talk vaguely about when we were nineteen. It's easy for me to picture us being together when we're as old as Ethel and Herbie."

She couldn't help a small smile.

She could picture it, too.

"On one hand," he said, "I'm angry we wasted so much time apart, but maybe it was necessary for me to be sure of who I am and what I want. We were quite young when we dated, after all." He paused. "I hope you feel the same way, but if not, I understand."

Two nights ago, she'd told Greg that she wanted to just *know* she had the right guy.

And now, she did.

He was the one for her.

That had been her Christmas wish: to figure out if she loved Greg in a way that would last. Her thoughts about second chances had been changing since her talk with her mother yesterday, but now...

Tasha was overwhelmed by her feelings. They had returned in full force, stronger than before, with a decade and a half of experience behind them. There was no way this could be wrong, not when it felt so perfect.

She set down her hot chocolate on a flat patch of snow, then reached into her jacket and held up the necklace she was wearing. For a moment, she simply looked at him and smiled. It felt like she was smiling from every inch of her body.

"I feel the same way," she said. "You know, I once got back together with an ex, and it didn't go well—we still had the same problems as before. I swore I'd never do it again. A couple of my friends got back together with their exes, too, and those relationships didn't work out, either. That's why I was reluctant to start anything with you. But it's different for you and me—I don't think it's foolish to say that. Before, we weren't quite in the right place in our lives for each other, but that's changed, plus we know ourselves better than we did as teenagers. I'm positive we can deal with any challenges that come our way. When I..." Now it was her turn to have trouble getting the words out. It had been many years since she'd said these words to a man. To her family, sure, but this wasn't the same.

So many years of wondering whether she'd ever meet the right guy, and it turned out she'd known him since kindergarten.

"When I was younger, I couldn't appreciate how special and rare this is, but I do now. I love you, Greg."

His arms came around her. "I love you, too."

There was a frustrating amount of fabric between them. Unfortunately, it was necessary, given the freezing temperature, but she was still glad he'd done this here. In a snow castle.

If someone had told her last week that on Christmas morning, she'd be romanced by Greg Wong in a snow castle, she wouldn't have believed them.

She pressed her lips to his. Unlike their very first kiss, in this very same park, she now knew what she was doing. She'd kissed many men in the intervening years, and that didn't make this mean less; it made her more certain that he was the right man. She'd truly never felt like this with anyone else.

His mouth moved over hers, urgent and firm, and she kissed him back with equal fervor, trying to get as close to him as she could with all their winter clothes in the way.

She'd never expected her future to involve embracing the past.

But she couldn't be happier.

"I'm glad I was twenty-seven minutes late on Monday," she said. "If I'd been on time, it might have all happened differently. Maybe we wouldn't have needed to spend the night in a cold motel room." She paused. "No regrets."

No regrets about the past couple days. No regrets about walking away from each other all those years before—she wouldn't let herself think about the what-ifs, only look forward to their future together. Perhaps Greg was right: they'd needed that time apart.

She kissed him again. So simple—her lips and tongue moving over his, but it was exquisite. She would get to do this again…and again…and again, and that filled her with warmth.

"I'm planning to stay in Mosquito Bay until the twenty-eighth," Greg said, "since I have more than a week off. Will you let me drive you back to Toronto? You can play all the Christmas music you like."

"No, I won't torture you like that. We can listen to CBC Radio for half the trip. Hopefully, we won't get stuck in a snowstorm this time, and when we get to your condo—"

"Perhaps I could ask you to watch Netflix and chill?"

She couldn't contain her laughter.

It was Christmas, and she was in love, and she was so full of joy.

"Or I could ask you to come upstairs and see my model train?" he suggested.

"I *would* like to see it. I'm curious." She picked up her hot chocolate and had a sip. "I'll come upstairs, see your model train, then head home on the subway."

"That's a terrible plan."

"Or maybe I could stick around for half an hour and you could make me a cup of tea."

"I suppose."

"Or you could bend me over the table where you keep your model train—"

"I don't like that idea at all," he said.

"Why not?"

"I don't want anything to happen to it, and surely you would mess it up. You have a tendency to, ah, move around quite a bit when you come. Better to bend you over the couch or the kitchen counter."

"I can accept those alternatives." She winked at him, then reached for another chocolate chip cookie. It was the best cookie she'd ever tasted.

"Greg!" someone shouted from outside the fort. "What is happening in there? Did you make up and kiss?"

Tasha assumed that was his grandma.

"Yeah, can we go home now?" That was probably Amber, Greg's younger sister, who'd been in elementary school fifteen years ago, but she'd be grown up now, too.

"Have you guys been standing out there the whole time?" Greg asked, but probably not loud enough for his family to hear.

"We're all good!" Tasha shouted. "You can leave now, thank you!"

There was round of applause, as though more people than just Greg's family had been standing around the snow fort, and Greg ducked his head in embarrassment.

"Dear God," he muttered.

"I just want everyone to know that I made this happen," Greg's mom said. "I'm taking full credit for this match."

"I spent hours out here yesterday freezing my ass off and listening to Greg boss me around." This must be Zach. "I want some credit, too."

"Same here," Nick said.

"Alright, we hear you," Greg said, loudly this time. "Now you can leave us in peace. I'll see you at dinner."

There were sounds of boots crunching through the snow, and then it was quiet once more. A red cardinal chirped from a nearby tree. Tasha might not know as much about birds as Greg, but she could identify a few.

"I'm having Christmas dinner with my family," he said, "and I'm sure you have plans with yours. But I still have a little time before then."

"Hmm. What could we possibly do with all that time? I have no idea."

"Don't you?" he murmured as he set aside her hot chocolate and gestured her inside the sleeping bags. He'd zipped two together.

Ooh, this was cozy.

He slid a camping pillow under her head. He was prepared for everything. Then he shed his winter jacket and climbed into the sleeping bags with her. His leg brushed against hers, and that nearly made her breathless.

"Who knew that being thirty-four would means lots of sex in a snow fort?" she said.

"Oh, are we having sex? I thought we were going to snuggle."

"We'll snuggle afterward."

And that's exactly what they did.

At ten o'clock that night, Tasha was cuddled up with Greg on the couch in her parents' living room. Greg had come over after dinner, figuring her parents' house would be quieter than his, now that her brothers and their families had left. As fun as the snow fort had been, it was nice to have some time together indoors.

Tasha had texted Monique earlier, and Monique, though she grudgingly admitted the photos of the snow fort were impressive, was aghast that Tasha was getting back together with her ex. Tasha was confident she'd made the right choice, though, and she was also confident Greg would win her friend over soon enough.

Greg clasped Tasha's hand, and their iron rings—which they both wore because they were engineers—rubbed against each other.

He lifted a gift box out of a bag he'd brought with him.

"Is that what I think it is?" she asked, one hand coming to her mouth.

He nodded. "You kept your necklace, and I kept these."

She'd been such a romantic that for their first Valentine's Day together, she'd given him an entire box of valentines.

He opened the box, and she picked up the first one, a heart that said, *Will you be my valentine?*

She smiled and set it down. "Will you be mine for Christmas, Greg?"

"There's nothing I want more."

Epilogue

Greg woke up to someone sliding her hands over his chest, and he smiled. He loved waking up next to Tasha.

It was January 25, one month since Christmas, one month since he'd declared his feelings for her in a snow fort in Mosquito Bay. The snow fort had started to melt when the weather warmed up a few days later, but their relationship was a different matter.

"Good morning," she murmured. "When do we have to leave?"

It was Chinese New Year today, and they were going back to Mosquito Bay to have dinner with his family. Tomorrow, they would visit hers.

He checked the clock. It was eight.

"No rush," he said. "Although if it takes as long to get there as last time, we won't make it for dinner tonight."

"True, but I don't think there's any danger of that."

Yes, since there was no snow in the forecast, their drive should be fine.

The past month had been wonderful. Familiar and new all at the same time. They frequently spent the night together, and waking up with her never got old.

They were planning to move in together soon. Likely, she would move into his place, and then they would look at buying a house, hopefully by next Christmas.

They were making plans for their future together, and he loved it.

When her hand slipped under his shirt, he grunted. A grunt of pleasure—as Tasha would know. Perhaps they could stay in bed a little longer before they got on with their day.

"Zach's bringing a girlfriend," he said. "Did I tell you?"

"No. I didn't know he was seeing anyone."

"I didn't either, until yesterday. It's lucky for him, though. My family had talked about setting him up again. Actually..."

Now that Greg thought about it, perhaps Zach didn't have a girlfriend and had just convinced a woman to come as his date so his parents wouldn't set him up with anyone. Perhaps this was a *fake* girlfriend.

Greg considered the possibility for a minute, then dismissed it.

No, a fake girlfriend for Chinese New Year seemed a bit extreme. His imagination must be running away with itself again.

He turned over so he was facing Tasha and grinned.

Usually, he hated it when people changed their plans on him, but rekindling his relationship with Tasha hadn't been in the plans, and he was very glad it had happened.

Now, his plan was to be with her for always.

And maybe have a little fun in this warm, queen-size bed before they got on the road.

About the Author

Jackie Lau decided she wanted to be a writer when she was in grade two, sometime between writing "The Heart That Got Lost" and "The Land of Shapes." She later studied engineering and worked as a geophysicist before turning to writing romance novels. Jackie lives in Toronto with her husband, and despite living in Canada her whole life, she hates winter. When she's not writing, she enjoys gelato, gourmet donuts, cooking, hiking, and reading on the balcony when it's raining.

To learn more and sign up for her newsletter, visit jackielaubooks.com.

Also by Jackie Lau

Love, Lies, and Cherry Pie

Donut Fall in Love Series
Donut Fall in Love
The Stand-Up Groomsman

Weddings with the Moks Series
Four Weddings to Fall in Love
Three Reasons to Run

Chu's Restaurant Series
The Sitcom Star
The Reluctant Heartthrob

Kwan Sisters/Fong Brothers Series
Grumpy Fake Boyfriend
Mr. Hotshot CEO
Pregnant by the Playboy
Bidding for the Bachelor

Cider Bar Sisters Series
Her Big City Neighbor
His Grumpy Childhood Friend
Her Pretend Christmas Date (novella)
The Professor Next Door
Her Favorite Rebound
Her Unexpected Roommate

Holidays with the Wongs Series
A Match Made for Thanksgiving
A Second Chance Road Trip for Christmas
A Fake Girlfriend for Chinese New Year
A Big Surprise for Valentine's Day

Baldwin Village Series

One Bed for Christmas (prequel novella)

The Ultimate Pi Day Party

Ice Cream Lover

Man vs. Durian

Chin-Williams Series

Not Another Family Wedding

He's Not My Boyfriend